Strip Mall Mysteries

Book One:

A Body to Die For

By Shannon Iwanski

Cover Design: TatteredWolf Studios
Interior Design: Shannon Iwanski

ISBN-10: 0692346791
ISBN-13: 978-0692346792

Also available in eBook format at Amazon.com

First Edition

Dedication

This novel is dedicated to my husband, Brent Iwanski, who never fails to show me support in all that I do. He deserves far more than mere words on a page.

Chapter One

"You can do this. Just get out of the car and go inside."

Max had been engaged in the same mental pep talk for over ten minutes, but the door on his Jeep stayed closed, and his body remained firmly planted in the cloth-covered seat. Barbados was supposed to take away all the anxiety and the stress from his break-up with Bobby. And it had while he had been there. Unfortunately, he had to come back—whether he wanted to or not—and all that avoidance had latched onto his back like a hyena on a zebra leg.

"This would be easier if *I* had dumped *him*." He groaned and drummed his hands on the steering wheel. The howling wind gusted over the Jeep, causing him to involuntarily shiver.

The clock showed 7:30am. The gym would be open in a half hour, and, if it was a typical Saturday, it would be slam packed with people ready to work out before window shopping in the rest of the strip mall.

"They all know we're not together anymore." He groaned again, drawing it out so pathetically long it became annoying to him. "There are going to be so many attempts to console me, the man stupid enough to let the hottest hunk in Tulsa get away."

His cell phone chimed, interrupting his pity party with a short, sweet melody. He thumbed the Galaxy's screen. Speak of the devil.

Welcome back. When will you be in?

He tossed the phone into the passenger seat and stared at the flickering sign above the gym. The first 'I' in Tight/Fit needed to be replaced. *My job,* he thought.

He breathed deeply, held it in, and grabbed the handle. The door opened more quickly than he intended, broke from his grasp, and slammed into a small decorative tree that had long since lost its leaves. Cursing himself silently, Max stepped out to survey the damage. The resulting dent got added to the pile of things going wrong with his life and the pile of things he had to do.

Or not. He slowly moved the door back and forth to judge the size and depth of the blemish. No chipped paint. It could wait.

The door slammed shut two seconds before he remembered he had left his cell phone behind and... *God!* He leaned his head against the chilly glass, staring at the small bundle of keys on his seat. *Bobby has a spare.*

Max whipped around, staring at the front door. *Just do it. Just go knock on the door, look stupid, and get this over with. Just go. Just go.*

After trudging to the gym's entrance, he discovered Bobby wasn't at the front desk. Max waited a few minutes, peering this way and that through the glass doors. Finally, he knocked a couple of times, gently rapping his knuckle against the glass. He knew the half-hearted attempt wouldn't accomplish anything but keep him from the inevitable.

Max exhaled a puff of air. Its fogginess reminded him of pretending to smoke on bitterly cold mornings when he was a kid. His shoulders sagged when his thoughts returned to the present.

The door shook as he pounded his palm against it. On the third strike, he misjudged and flung his fingers into the metal outlining the glass. He shoved the hand between his legs, cursing and dancing around.

That was when Bobby decided to show himself.

"Of course," he muttered.

Max stopped, staring at his ex through the glass. A sheepish smile crawled across his lips, and he used his undamaged hand to wave lamely. Bobby unlocked the door, holding it open.

"Hey, there you are." Bobby's warm, infectious smile melted Max's heart the way it always did. "I was wondering when you would get here. Come on in."

Max didn't budge. He pulled his hand from between his legs and inspected the angry redness covering his two outer fingers. "I, um, locked my keys in the car." He mumbled, hoping Bobby wouldn't really hear him, even though he had no alternative.

"I put my key on your desk. Want me to get it for you?" Bobby asked.

"Sure. Thanks." Max held the door open, forcing himself to not watch Bobby walk away or jog back.

"Here you go. See you in a few minutes. I want to talk to you about something before we open." Bobby handed him the key, smiled, and went back to their shared office.

"I can do this. I *can* do this," Max told himself all the way to the car and back. The words offered no comfort, and he didn't believe them for a second, but it was better than screaming. Although, *that* would help.

He smelled the vanilla candle long before he stepped through the door to his and Bobby's office. Too many memories suddenly needed to be tamped down, and he did it with the biggest mental shovel he could find: anger.

"Do you have to burn that all the time? It stinks the whole place up." He tossed his keys on the desk and fell into his chair without looking at the target of his verbal barrage.

"I'm glad you're back, Max. I missed you, too," Bobby deadpanned as he picked up the metal lid and snapped it onto the candle without blowing it out. "You're looking good. Nice tan. How was the weather? Better than Oklahoma in winter, I bet."

"Yep." Max turned on his computer and looked at the clock on the wall. *Fifteen more minutes*, he thought. "You still teaching eight o'clock Pilates?"

"Yes." If the lack of conversation upset Bobby, he did an excellent job of hiding it. He didn't sound the least bit frustrated.

"Good. I want to finish up the books for the month. We need to fix the sign. Did you let anything else fall apart while I was gone?" The computer finished its boot cycle. Max suddenly found himself staring at the picture of him and Bobby kissing at their last anniversary party. *Our* last *anniversary.*

He quickly turned the monitor off. "Well, I could have done without that," he sighed.

"Max, are you sure you can do this?"

"What does that mean?" He hadn't intended to shout. One breath, two breaths, and...three breaths. *That didn't help.*

Bobby's hands were flat on the desk in front of him. He leaned back in his chair. The smile had disappeared.

"I mean," he said in a measured tone, "do you want to stay partners—business partners? Or, do you want me to buy your half, and you can do something else?"

"You'd like that, wouldn't you?" *What are you doing, crazy man?* Max couldn't believe his own ears. *This is stupid. Stop it.* "No, I don't want to sell. Just because you can turn your back on everything we worked for and built up from nothing doesn't mean that I can do the same thing."

"I didn't—" Bobby cut himself off. His hands had clenched into fists that could probably turn coal to diamonds. "I know this is hard for you. I'm sorry. If this is going to be a problem for you, maybe we should try a different arrangement."

Max propped his elbows on his desk and buried his face in his hands, scrubbing until he saw brilliant flashes of light behind his eyelids. "It's not going to be a problem."

"Are you sure? Because—"

"Not a problem," he spat. Another deep breath did exactly nothing to quench the emotional fire. "I can do this. I will do this. It will take time. I'm sure it would be easier if I didn't still love you."

"I still love you, too, Max," Bobby said softly. "I'm just not in—"

Max glared at Bobby, killing the words before they sprang to life. "Robert Sampson, as God is my witness, if you tell me one more time that you are not *in* love with me, I am going to wrap my hands in your luxurious auburn hair, and I am going to beat your gorgeous face into that desk until your perfect smile looks like the front end of a rusted Mack truck. Do you understand what I'm saying?" *God! What* am *I saying?*

Bobby nodded.

"Good. Now, you said you wanted to talk to me. If it was to tell me the unspeakable thing, this conversation is over. If not, please, go on." Max leaned back in his chair, arms crossed over his chest. The long, metallic squeak battering his ear drums got thrown on the 'fix-it' pile.

"Maybe now isn't—"

"Now."

"Dang it, Max, will you stop interrupting me?" Bobby stood up and paced back and forth behind his desk. No easy feat, since he could only take three steps in each direction. "I need... I need to know you're okay. That we're okay. I honestly do love you. I hated hurting you. You've been gone for two months, and I know that isn't really a long time, but it doesn't seem like you've started dealing with this at all. You're angry."

"Well, excuuuuuuse me."

"Now, now, I'm not trying to pick." Bobby held his hand out, most likely to stop the next verbal flood. "I'm just stating facts. If this is going to work, we can't be fighting all the time. You can't be so caustic. That's not like you. It doesn't look good on you. You'll get wrinkles."

Max scoffed, involuntarily running a hand over his forehead. He flipped Bobby off and tried very hard not to smile or laugh.

"Uh huh. I knew I could appeal to your vanity, if nothing else." Bobby's pacing led him to the door. He leaned against the jamb, unintentionally looking like an underwear model at a photo shoot. "I'm serious, though, Maximillianaire, I can't do this if it destroys us both, destroys our souls. I'll walk away before I let that happen."

"Please don't call me that." The words came out in a tight whisper tinged with the threat of angry tears.

"But I've always called you Maximillianaire, even before we started dating. I can't stop now, even if I wanted to."

Max shook his head. He didn't want to believe that Bobby was being sincere, but there was no denying the tone of his voice.

Damn him for being so charming. God, how did I let him get away?

No, stop doing that. Time to start fresh. Start new.

He sighed. "I'm sorry about being so cranky. You're right. I didn't face any of this in Barbados. I just stayed drunk."

"I'm going to go unlock the doors," Bobby said. "I know you want to get at the books—and change your desktop pic—but will you walk with me? I have one more thing to tell you."

"Sure." Max followed him from the office and waited in the main reception area. Four people approached the door at the same time, smiling and waving at Bobby, who held the door for them. Max struggled to not laugh at Elizabeth Walker, who gave Bobby the once-over like always.

"Max, glad you're back." Her tone said the opposite, as usual

"Thanks, Elizabeth." Max put as much cheer and pep into his voice as he could, partly to stop himself from throttling her and partly because he knew it irked her. "Nice to see you, too. Class will start shortly."

"Thanks." She walked past without even a second glance at him.

He greeted the other early-birds and fell in step with Bobby. "That woman wants to eat you for breakfast, lunch, *and* dinner."

They laughed. *Maybe I can do this,* Max thought.

"So, a lot has happened since you've been gone," Bobby said. He flipped on the lights in rooms along the main hall as they walked past. "I've hired someone to help out around here. I didn't know when you'd be back, and I couldn't run the place alone. I hope you don't mind."

"Not at all. Do you think we can afford to keep the person on, now that I'm back?" Max asked.

"Well, I hope so. You see, I, um, well..."

Here it comes, Max thought. "Just tell me. Who is it?"

"Skylar Pratt." Bobby flinched.

"What?! You let that little punk in here? I'm surprised he hasn't stolen the light fixtures so he can pawn them to buy drugs." Max couldn't wrap his mind around Bobby sometimes. "What were you thinking?"

"I was thinking he needed help, and I could give it to him." Bobby had gone on the defensive, and Max could tell from that alone there was worse to come.

"Please tell me you didn't."

Bobby clamped his lips shut for a moment. "We've been dating for a few weeks," he said softly.

"You've been dating Skylar Pratt?" Max shouted.

"Shhh. Keep your voice down." Bobby stared to the end of the hall, checking if anyone had heard.

"Don't you shush me." Max felt the fire bubbling up from his stomach. "How could you date that little low-life? My God, Bobby, he's had more drugs and needles in him than a Wal-Mart pharmacy. What were you thinking?"

"You already asked me that, and I told you I was thinking I could help him out. Help him get clean." Bobby looked down at his shoes. "And I was...lonely."

"I hope you got tested," Max said.

"We haven't done anything. It's innocent."

"That word has never been applied to Skylar," Max scoffed.

"Look, I know you're mad, but this is how things are now," Bobby said. "And I want you to be nice to Skylar, especially since he's just getting over a very nasty virus. He's been puking and running a fever for a couple days, not to mention bad stomach cramps. So, please, just promise me—"

Both men's heads turned toward a banshee shriek. Running as fast as they could, they rounded the corner at the end of the hall.

A few feet away, Elizabeth Walker bounced up and down outside the door to the sauna, screaming like she'd seen the ghosts of a million mice.

Max pulled her away, escorting her to a plastic chair. From a small ice chest nearby, he retrieved a bottle of water and thrust it into Elizabeth's hands, encouraging her to drink. She interrupted her hysterics long enough to gulp some down.

"There you go. You're okay." From how badly she was shaking and sloshing water onto the floor, he knew she wasn't. "Wait here. I'm going to see if Bobby needs me."

"Don't," Bobby said behind him.

Max looked up at him. He had never seen anyone look so pale. Bobby grabbed his arm and pulled him off to the side.

"Did she see more than she bargained for?" Max had meant it to be a joke, but the look on Bobby's face killed the attempt at humor.

"You could say that," Bobby said softly. He leaned against the wall and slowly slid down until he landed on his knees. He stroked his face from mouth to chin several times before looking up at Max and saying, "It's Skylar. He's dead."

Chapter Two

"Here, sweetie, drink this. It's a new blend I'm trying out made from Arabica and green coffee beans. That should pep you right up."

Max accepted the tan mug from Kandy Morrell and moved it back and forth beneath his nose. "Smells delicious. Thanks so much for letting me in early. I couldn't stay there another minute."

"Any time, Max, you know that. Mind Your Own Beans is open for you whenever you need it. Heaven knows you've been there for me more times than I care to admit." She pulled her legs up and tucked them beneath herself in the black leather chair beside his. The steam from her own cup of Joe skirted along the perimeter of her face and dissipated into the air.

"I knew Skylar was going to die eventually, but I didn't think it would be in my sauna. I think it cooked him." He shuddered.

"How's Bobby handling it?"

He lowered the cup from his lips and stared at her. "So you know about them, huh?"

She leaned back almost like she wanted to distance herself from him. "Yes, Bobby told me. And just because the two of you were together for seven years doesn't mean he can't find love with someone else."

"What are two months compared to seven *years*?" Max demanded. He drowned and scalded more words with a hasty gulp of coffee he instantly regretted. Brown liquid sloshed onto the table as he hastily sat the cup down.

"Careful," Kandy chided gently. "Don't hurt yourself out of spite."

"It's not spite." He glared at her. "I can't believe Bobby hooked up with *Skylar Pratt*, of all people. He could have any man in the world."

"We all heal in our own times, in our own ways. Bobby heals himself by fixing other people's wounds," Kandy said. "You need to start working on you because if what I'm seeing is any indication, this break up is destroying you. This isn't the Max I know and love."

"I hate you." He smiled at her wicked laughter and pulled away before she could punch him in the arm. "You're right. Of course, you're right. You always are. I think the best way for me to start healing is to focus on the gym."

"Let's go back to the part about me being right," she said with a wink.

He rolled his eyes and gingerly sipped from the still-hot liquid. The sound of the bell on the front door caught his and Kandy's attention. Looking up, he saw a familiar, handsome face walking through the front door.

The tall, lanky man scanned the coffee shop before locking his blue eyes on Max and walking toward him. Max smiled briefly, but it fell when it wasn't returned.

"Willie Harris. It's been a long time." Max made no effort to hide taking stock of the man. Well-groomed blondish-brown hair. Decent suit. Highly-polished shoes. A preferable change from the gawky young man with stained sneakers and baggy jean shorts he'd been in college.

"It's William, please. Actually, *Detective* Harris for the time being." Max caught a hint of the old awkwardness peeking from beneath Harris's words.

He stood up and shook hands. "Detective, this is Kandy Morrell."

"Ma'am."

"Nice to meet you, Detective. Would you like a cup of coffee?"

"Please." He waited for her to walk away before assuming her seat. "It's good to see you again, Max. Unfortunately, it has to be this way, and I have to ask you some questions."

"I understand. It's good to see you again, too. We have lots to catch up on. After," he added hastily. "Have you already talked to Bobby?"

"Yes, but I can't tell you what we discussed. I'm sure you'll understand." He barely waited for Max's head to start nodding before asking, "Where were you this morning?"

Max gave him the shortened version, leaving out the dithering in his car and the discussions before Elizabeth Walker went ballistic. "Skylar may not have been the best apple in the bunch, but he didn't deserve to die like that."

"Like what?" Harris asked.

"You know..." He waved his hand vaguely in the air. "...cooked."

"I'm pretty sure the sauna didn't kill him. That just finished the job. Can you tell me who might have wanted to kill Mr. Pratt?"

Max processed the words. "You're saying he was murdered?"

"That's how it appears." Harris stared intently at him.

"Well, knowing Skylar, half of north Tulsa probably wanted him dead. He was always into someone for drugs, or money, or both." Max shook his head, and finished the last of his coffee.

"Perfect timing." Kandy grabbed his cup, set it on the tray in her hand, and placed two fresh, full mugs on the table. "Let me know if you need anything else."

Both men thanked her.

"So, what kind of drugs are we talking about?" Harris asked.

"The list of drugs he *didn't* take would probably be shorter," Max said. "Mostly it was pot and heroin, but there were others, I'm sure. I can't believe Bobby was willing to get himself mixed up in all that."

"What do you mean?" Harris asked. He narrowed his eyes. "Was your partner getting involved in drugs?"

"Ex-partner. Business partner. We recently broke up."

"Oh, I'm sorry," Harris said.

"Bobby wasn't getting into drugs." Max put all of his heart-felt conviction into the words he had no doubts about. "He was trying to get Skylar out of them, and most likely falling in love with him at the same time. No way would Bobby ever do drugs. Have you seen his body?"

"Yes."

"Then you can believe me when I say he wouldn't do anything to undo all the hard work he's put into it," Max said.

"Was anyone else in the building this morning?" Harris asked.

"I think it was just the three of us, but I had no idea that Skylar was there until Elizabeth Walker started screaming."

"So, as far as you know, Bobby and Skylar were alone in the gym before you came in?" Harris asked.

"As far as I know," Max said. Slowly the realization hit him. "But Bobby wouldn't have killed Skylar. He had no reason to do it, especially if he was working half as hard as I suspect he was in getting Skylar clean."

"I guess we'll find out, won't we?" Harris took a drink of the coffee, sighed appreciatively, and said, "I want you to come back to the gym with me and answer a few more questions."

Max groaned and nodded. He retrieved two paper cups and lids from the counter and transferred his and Harris's coffee. Kandy came from the kitchen to retrieve the empty mugs, kissed Max on the cheek, and told him to come back later. She sent him off with a squeeze on the shoulder.

Outside, Max shivered in the sudden, biting wind, longing for the warm beaches of Barbados. "God, I hate winter."

"It could be worse," Harris chuckled. "At least we aren't skating on ice."

Max nodded in understanding. "So, what happened with you after college? Well, I mean, obviously you're a cop, but what else?"

"I traveled a lot; I had to find myself. Corny, I know, but true." Harris shrugged his shoulders. "I had to rid myself of all the baggage I was carrying. The academy helped with that."

"I wish you had stayed in touch."

"I'm sorry I didn't," Harris said. "Depression nearly got the best of me several times. At the least I should have told you how much your friendship meant to me. How much it helped when I didn't think I'd make it one more day."

"Sure you would have. You had this person in you all along. He just needed time to shine through." Max side-stepped a concrete planter and accidentally bumped into Harris.

"Careful. Assaulting a police officer is a felony," Harris joked.

"I'll keep that in mind."

The walk from Mind Your Own Beans to Tight/Fit was short but still enough to almost completely sap the warmth from Max's body. He rushed into the main area, thanked Harris for holding the door, and rubbed his arms vigorously.

"You ready for this?" Harris asked.

"Not really, but I don't think it matters," Max said. "Lead on, Detective. The sooner we start the sooner I can start damage control on our reputation. If I know Elizabeth Walker, half of Tulsa already knows what happened this morning."

They stopped in front of the sauna. Bobby was nowhere to be seen. Max assumed he was being questioned somewhere away from the crime scene. He turned his head while two men wheeled a shrouded gurney out of the sauna and down the hall.

"You okay?" Harris asked. He gently rested his hand on Max's shoulder.

"I will be. So, um, questions," he prompted.

"Right." The detective cleared his throat. "Tell me what happened when you and Bobby found the body."

Max went through the details, explaining his attempts to calm Elizabeth Walker while Bobby went into the sauna to determine what had caused her outburst.

"So he went in alone?"

"Yes."

"Did anyone touch the body?"

"Not that I know of," Max said. "But I can't say that for sure because like I said, I was out here."

"When did you get back from your trip?"

"Last night around ten o'clock. I went home, went to bed, and then got up early this morning so I could talk to Bobby before we opened." Realization struck Max. "Do you think I killed Skylar?"

"Did you?"

Max laughed. "I've been accused of being many things in my life, but this is the first time murderer has been thrown out there."

"I'm just asking questions," Harris said. "It's not an accusation, and that wasn't a denial."

"I didn't do it. I had no idea Bobby and Skylar were an item until this morning, and I try to make it a habit to stay as far away from Skylar as possible." Max knew he was telling the truth, but he couldn't stop the nagging feeling that he didn't sound convincing enough.

Harris nodded several times while digging in an inside pocket of his suit jacket. He handed Max a card. "Here's my number. If you remember anything else or think of anything I should know, call me."

"I will," Max said. He tucked the card into his pocket. "So, if you're finished with questions, I'm going to go find Bobby and see how he's doing."

"Don't bother."

Max turned around and saw his ex and a police officer walking from the main workout room a short distance away.

"What's going on?" Max demanded of anyone willing to answer the question.

"He's just coming in for some routine questioning," Harris said. "*If* he didn't kill Skylar Pratt, he has nothing to worry about."

Chapter Three

"I told you, Bobby didn't do this," Max said.

"Unfortunately, I can't just take your word for it." Max saw apology in Harris's eyes. "But I wish I could."

"So do I," Max whispered. He had to sit down. The coolness of the plastic chair seeped into his legs and gave him a strange sense of comfort. *What do I do? I know Bobby didn't kill Skylar. But who did? God, who* wouldn't *want to kill him?*

"I'm finished with my part of the investigation here. The Medical Examiner left with Skylar's body. Once all my men clear out, you can re-open whenever you want," Harris said. He stood beside Max, far enough away for breathing room, but close enough for comfort.

"Re-open." Max repeated the word hollowly, not sure if it even made sense. "I don't think we'll do that today. I need more time…and answers."

"Oh, who hired *the strippers*?!"

The shrill voice cut through Max's eardrums like an axe through rotten wood. He looked up at the man staring at all the policemen. Undoubtedly, he was undressing them all in his mind.

"Corey, could you go be a cliché somewhere else, please? And if you could be someone other than yourself, I would appreciate that, too," Max said. He wanted to keep the anger to a minimum, but he knew it wasn't necessary. *The little queen doesn't have the sense to know when to be civil.*

True to form, Corey seemed unfazed by what Max had said. Instead, he sidled up beside Detective Harris and went through the motions of fighting to restrain himself from running a finger along the detective's suit sleeve.

"Hi, I'm Corey Barnes. I run the juice bar here. Can I interest you in something? I have a *huge* selection of things that aren't on the menu." He smiled and winked.

"I'd be interested to know where you were this morning between seven and eight o'clock," Harris said. He pushed away from the wall he'd been leaning on and crossed his arms over his chest.

"Oh, you're naughty. I like that, honey." Corey mimicked Harris, crossing his own arms, but he added a hip thrust to the side and swiveled back and forth like a washing machine on the gentle cycle. "Well, I was kind of tied—"

"Corey!" Max stood up so quickly the chair slammed back into the wall, leaving a dent in the drywall. "This is no time for games. Skylar is *dead*. They think Bobby did it. Be serious for once and just answer his question." The crest-fallen look on Corey's face stabbed Max in the heart.

"I'm sorry. I didn't know," Corey whispered. He thumped into the wall and slid to the floor, resting his chin on his knees. "Is he really dead?"

"Yes," Harris said. "Where were you this morning?"

"I was with someone I met at The Tool Box. I just left a few minutes ago."

Harris wrote down the information for Corey's alibi. Max felt badly for Corey and hated how he had snapped at him, but Corey never took anything seriously. He just counted on his youth, looks, and body to carry him through any situation, regardless of social norms.

Max heard Harris tell Corey he would be in touch. Corey stayed on the floor, staring straight ahead, while Max and Harris walked off a bit to talk.

"I'm sure his alibi will check out," Max said. "He isn't one for making up things about guys."

Harris looked back at Corey. "I honestly don't think he did it, but I still have to check it out."

"What's wrong?" Max asked. He was sure he had seen a tell-tale sign of doubt flash across the detective's face.

"It's nothing," Harris said. He turned back, obviously forcing a smile. "I think I have everything I need. I'll talk to you later."

"Yeah." Max shook hands and watched the detective leave. When he was out of sight, Max rushed to Corey. "What did you tell him, other than the contact info for your latest conquest?"

Corey looked up through tear-stained, puffy eyes. "I just answered some questions. You heard everything I said."

"There's something else going on," Max said. "A cop doesn't look at someone the way he just looked at you unless wheels are turning. Do you know anything you're not telling?"

"No." Corey shook his head and dashed tears from his eyes with the heels of his hands. "I can't believe Skylar is dead. Did they notify his family, or take his stuff? This is terrible."

"You let them worry about all that," Max said, narrowing his eyes at Corey. "You go home, but be back tomorrow for your regular shift."

"What about—"

"You'll get paid for today, don't worry," Max said. "Corey, seriously, if there is *anything* else you need to tell me, please, do it now."

Corey shook his head. "There's nothing, Max. I swear." He stood up, took a deep breath. "I'm going to go get my bag out of the locker room. I'll see you tomorrow."

Max nodded and told Corey to call if he needed anything. He watched the young man walk toward the locker room. He had almost convinced himself he was suspicious for no reason when Corey looked over his shoulder.

Max couldn't be certain, but he was pretty sure the look that had been on Harris's face was now on his own, too. *Come on, Max. You're just paranoid. Please just be paranoid.* He hurried to the door and pushed it open, thankful he kept the hinges in good repair. They didn't squeak, and that gave him an opportunity to sneak in unannounced.

The staff lockers were in the far corner of the room. He walked past the first free-standing row. A locker door slammed shut quickly followed by the sound of another one opening and closing. Max stopped at the end of the next row, peeking around the corner.

The door to the hallway was slowly closing.

He walked quickly to Skylar's locker and pulled it open. Empty. He couldn't be sure the police hadn't removed everything, but he would bet the gym on his certainty that Corey had been in it.

I don't know what he's doing, but I'm going to find out. Max left the locker room behind, intent on catching up to Corey. *Hopefully I'm just making more out of this than I should be.*

He cut through the large room with all the free-standing equipment and emerged into the hallway by his and Bobby's office. A short dash to the exit revealed Corey's car was still sitting in its usual spot, but he wasn't in it.

A noise from the juice bar forced him to backtrack. Only half the lights had been turned on in the room. All the chairs were still on the tables. Corey kneeled beside a wet floor sign lying next to an overturned metal trash can.

"In a hurry?" Max asked.

"Oh, Jesus, you scared me to death!" Corey exclaimed. He pressed his palm against his chest, gulping air far too dramatically. "Why are you sneaking up on people?"

"I'm not sneaking up on anyone. Why the guilty conscience?" Max eyed him skeptically.

"Max, honey, I'm not guilty of anything but being young and attractive." Corey finished putting the last of the trash back in the can and made his way to the sink behind the juice bar to wash his hands.

"Where's your bag?" Max leaned against the bar, looking behind it.

Corey dried his hands and tossed his bag on the granite counter. "Are you accusing me of something? Well, here it is! Go through it if it makes you feel better." He put his hands on his hips and glared.

Max opened his mouth to say something and clamped it back shut. "I'm not accusing you of anything. You're just acting very strange."

"What do you expect? Skylar is dead. Bobby's probably going to jail if Mr. Sexy Detective Man has his way about it."

"Bobby didn't do it," Max protested.

Corey kept talking as if Max hadn't said a word. "I don't know what we're going to do. Let's face it, Max, you're the brains behind the operation, but Bobby is the heart, soul, face, and hot body. The two of us can't do this alone." Corey unzipped his bag and dumped the contents out.

Max quickly scanned the few items: a change of clothes, protein powder packets, two e-cigarettes, a glucometer, and three syringes.

"So you finally decided to quit smoking? That's good." Max put everything back into the bag. He couldn't miss Corey's large smile.

"Better?" Corey asked.

"Yes. And I wasn't accusing you of anything." Max sighed and sank into a tall stool. "This is all just so much to take in at once."

"I know. Here, you relax, and I'll fix you something to pep you up." Corey waved away Max's protest and set about concocting his famous energy drink. "So, how was Barbados?"

"I was too drunk to remember." He shared Corey's knowing laugh. "It was nice while I was there, but now I wish I had spent more time working through things. I'm walking around in the Twilight Zone."

"There are far worse places to be, honey, believe me." Corey dumped green nuclear waste into a tall glass and pushed it into Max's hands. "Drink up."

"People actually drink this mess?" Max asked. He eyed the glass suspiciously.

"It's a best seller; just don't ask what's in it." Corey winked.

Against his better judgment, Max sniffed the drink and slurped it. "Something that ugly should *not* taste so good," he said.

Corey smiled and smacked his palm on the counter. "Another satisfied customer. Now, what are we going to do, boss man?"

Max took another drink, stalling. "We're going to call in as many people as we can and run business as usual today. You take care of that. Since we're already here, we might as well. We'll just keep the sauna closed and put an 'Out of Order' sign on the door.

"I have to call our lawyer and put him on alert since I doubt Bobby is exercising his right." He gulped down the rest of the energy drink and pushed the cup toward Corey. "We can do this."

"Of course, we can." Corey dropped his bag on the floor and retrieved the cordless phone from its charging station on the wall. "Leave everything to me. Oh, and don't forget that you have to meet with the group tonight to go over their books."

Max groaned. "I forgot about that." He grabbed the cup and stared into its emptiness. "You mind fixing me another? I have a feeling I'm going to need it."

Corey patted Max's shoulder comfortingly. "Honey, once you see Eden's books, you're going to want me to fix an IV drip of that stuff."

Chapter Four

Max breathed deeply, held it, and slowly blew it out. He had spent most of the day on back-and-forth phone calls with the lawyer and Bobby's voicemail. *And now the real fun begins.* He tried to laugh but stifled it when it came out a groan.

He locked the front doors and turned off the "open" sign before systematically making his way through the rest of the gym, shutting off lights. The small bits of trash and cleaning could be left for the janitor on Sunday morning.

His route ended at the juice bar like always. Corey had already cleaned up the area and put everything in its place. *The little queen is flighty and fickle, but he's proud of what he does.*

True to his word, Corey had left a small disposable cup full of his energy concoction in the refrigerator. Max smiled at the note wishing him luck and downed a good portion of the green drink. He still couldn't reconcile in his mind how something that looked that disturbingly vile could taste so delicious.

After finishing the remainder, Max rinsed the cup and tossed it into the trash behind the counter. A dark object on the floor caught his eye. He stooped and retrieved one of Corey's vaping devices.

He probably doesn't even realize he lost this. Max shook his head and pushed the device into his pocket, intent on giving it back when he saw Corey next.

Turning out the last light in the juice bar, Max retrieved his laptop bag from the office and let himself out, locking the door behind. The sun had disappeared not long before, and the wind and temperature were taking advantage of the lack of even the slightest bit of heat.

Max shivered and wrapped his black and white scarf around his neck, winding it high enough to cover his mouth and nose. The gentle sounds of traffic traveling along I-44 washed over him. A peaceful winter night.

He resituated the bag by lifting the strap over his head to the opposite shoulder and started the dreaded trek back to Mind Your Own Beans. *Why did I come back just in time for end-of-the-month bookkeeping?*

He and Bobby had been the first to move into the new strip mall after it had been built five years before. They had been lucky enough to have connections with the building owner and rented the largest space before it had even been constructed. Slowly more people and businesses trickled in, and they had gotten to know and become friends with their new 'neighbors.'

Unfortunately for him everyone else found out he was a closet accountant, and one by one, they had persuaded him to do their books. *I guess it's not all bad. It* is *extra money, and as many cookies as Mrs. Gallowylde can cram down my throat.* He smiled at the thought of the older woman bouncing around, leaving saucers of sugar, milk, and honey out for the fairies she thought inhabited her store.

As he started to walk past Garden of Eden, he stopped and looked through the slightly frosted glass at a beautiful arrangement of roses. Eden Summers worked magic with plants and flowers. She could take a plant two steps from death's door and have it looking like a million dollars in no time.

Too bad she can't do the same thing with a budget. Max groaned as he remembered what Corey had said. Between the energy drink and whatever coffee he could get his hands on, he hoped it would be enough to get him through the trying ordeal of Eden's monthly accounts.

Kandy let him into her store. She greeted him with a kiss on the cheek and a hot cup of coffee that smelled amazing and warmed his hands. He heard the door lock behind him as he made his way to his usual table in the center of the room. The other business owners greeted him, welcoming him with comforting-but-knowing smiles.

Today was going to be worse than usual. *Death tends to make everything worse—no matter who dies.* He mentally chided himself for the unforgiving thought.

"Are you ready for me to unleash the hounds?" Kandy moved salt and pepper shakers and a napkin dispenser off of the table so he could set up his laptop. "I'm sure you know they're going to bombard you with talk about Skylar...and Bobby."

He sighed. "I know. The only way to get out of tonight is to fake my own death or a freak ice storm. This *is* Oklahoma, so that one isn't out of the realm of possibility."

"Who first?" she asked.

Max scanned the room. All eyes were on him, and he could tell they were chomping at the bit. "Let's start with Zane. His accounts are always in order. A small victory will give me strength to get through this." *I hope.*

The laptop started its boot cycle, and Max gingerly sipped the hot, black coffee. He removed his coat, draping it over the back of the wooden chair, and tossed his scarf on the table. His chair scraped noisily along the floor just as Zane Rogers sat beside him.

"Hey, Zane." He felt Corey's e-cig poking into his waist where it protruded from his pocket, so he pulled it out and set it on the table beside his scarf.

"Hello, Max. I'm glad you're back." Zane, a tall, nerdy beanpole, folded himself into his own chair. He had a way of making all furniture look like it belonged in a dollhouse. "You doing okay?"

"I'm good. You?" Max asked.

"Oh, you know." Zane placed a yellow manila folder on the table beside Max. "Everything is there for the past two months."

Max opened the folder and shuffled through the invoices and receipts. Zane's store, My Parents' Basement, specialized in comic books and rare collectibles. The man was a walking encyclopedia of nerd knowledge that spanned several decades. He also had good business sense, and his accounts always showed it.

"You finally sold that Predator statue, huh?" Max asked.

"Yeah. I forgot how hard it was to get that monster into the store. That's life-sized replicas for you, though. I'm just glad it's gone. That thing gave me the creeps." Zane chuckled.

"I'm sure the money more than makes up for that."

"Yes, sir. It does indeed," Zane said with a resolute nod.

Max opened his FastSheet software and found Zane's file. It only took a few minutes to update the information for two months. *Very glad I started this way. One down; five to go.*

"Ok, Zane, you're all set. Tell your wife I said hello. Oh, and thank her for the scarf." He indicated the garment lying on the table. "I love Michael Kors. She knows me too well."

"It's the least we could do after everything you and...um, you do for us." Zane turned red, and Max automatically filled in the stammer with Bobby's name.

"It's ok," Max whispered. "It's going to take time for all of us to adjust to."

"You ok?"

"I will be." Max hoped he wasn't lying. "Thanks for caring, Zane. I'll email you the latest FastSheet so you can file it."

"You're awesome." Zane shook his hand, retrieved the folder, and went to the counter to talk to Kandy.

No questions about Skylar. Maybe I'm worried for nothing.

"Oh, you poor dear. How are you holding up?" The sweet voice asking the dreaded question floated across the table from Henrietta Gallowylde.

"Henny, we talked about this. You're supposed to keep quiet. Remember?" Her husband, John, shook his head and slumped into the chair beside Max. "Sorry. I tried, but you know how that goes."

Max smiled and waved away the concern. "It's alright, John. It's only natural for people to be concerned or curious." Max turned his gaze to the old woman and fought to keep a natural smile on his lips. "Hello, Henrietta. I'm doing very well, thank you."

"That's not what my fairies say, Max, dear. They told me you've been very distraught. And now this terrible thing that happened to poor Skylar. It's just unimaginable." She shook her head and rubbed the small charm of a pixie she carried everywhere.

Max wished the fairies she talked about were a gaggle of gay men that constantly hovered around her bakery, Crumbles, but no such luck. She honestly believed she saw and talked to small, flying, mythological creatures that watched over her, her husband, and anyone she cared about, too. Her husband had long ago given up trying to dissuade her from the thought.

"Thank you for your concern. It's greatly appreciated." Before she could say anything else, Max turned to John and asked, "Do you have your file for me?"

Mr. Gallowylde handed the folder over with an understanding smile. "As always. Everything should be in order. The cost of fairy food is killing us, as usual."

"Jonathan, don't say it like that. If you upset them, they'll leave and never come back." Henny rubbed the charm more vigorously.

"Do you promise?" The old man mumbled the words softly. His wife either didn't hear or chose to ignore them.

"I'll see what I can do, John." Max went through the contents of the folder. He actively blocked out the sound of Henny's voice, but her request for a saucer of milk broke through his defenses.

Dutifully and without question, Kandy brought the requested order and placed it on the table beside the old woman. Max shook his head and wondered—not for the first time—what brought a person to the point Henrietta Gallowylde had reached. Corey said it was the death of her oldest son. Others were far less forgiving in their assessments and hypotheses.

One of these days she'll prove us all wrong when that milk actually disappears in front of our eyes. Max tried to suppress his smile, but it broke through anyway.

"Now, don't you worry, dear Max. I already have my darlings working on your man problem. They'll have you fixed up with someone else before you know it." The gleeful twinkle in her eyes melted Max.

"My God, Henrietta!" John exclaimed at the same time Max said, "Thank you. That's very sweet." Max looked at her husband and shrugged. "It's ok," he whispered.

"They helped Bobby. That young Skylar was so good for him. It gave him something to focus on and believe in again." She opened a sugar packet Kandy had brought—unasked—and poured the contents into the saucer of milk. "It's just too bad the poor dear is dead. And to think the police believe our Bobby could have done it. I'll have to send my darlings to the station to tell them that's not possible."

Max's hand darted out, grabbed ahold of John's, and squeezed it before the man could finish his inhalation of breath portending a verbal tirade the likes of which Mind Your Own Beans had never seen. John instantly deflated.

"Any help you can give is appreciated, as always, Henny." *It's not polite to kill old ladies. It's not polite to kill old ladies.* Max released John's hand. "So, you introduced Bobby and Skylar?"

"Oh, yes," she said in far too bubbly a manner for Max's mood. "My darlings pointed him out as soon as he came in one day. You know me; I like to work magic. I intentionally mixed up their orders and disappeared into the back so they had no choice but to interact. It worked like a charm."

"The kid was so drugged out of his mind he didn't realize he had a scone instead of a bear claw. Then he threw up everywhere." John shook his head, obviously still angry about the situation. "Bobby got mixed up with that loser, and look what it got him." He pointed his finger at Max. "That Bobby lost whatever sense he had when he left you. I don't know what got into him, but it wasn't anything intelligent, if you ask me."

I'm in gay hell. "Thanks for your support." Max focused on the FastSheet for Crumbles and entered the information as quickly as he could. After fifteen minutes of more fairy talk and defusing the atomic bomb slowly reaching critical mass inside Mr. Gallowylde,

Max sent them on their way. He promised to stop by for a dozen cookies on Monday morning.

If there's a God, the fairies will poison the cookies and put me out of my misery. Max looked at his watch. *Only 7:15? I* am *in hell.*

Kandy placed a fresh cup of coffee in front of him. "More go-juice. I've got a ham and cheese Panini ready to come out in a few minutes. Want some of the tomato and mozzarella salad to go with it?"

"Yes! You spoil me so much. Too bad you're not a man," he said.

"I get that all the time. Believe me, you couldn't handle me." She returned the wink and disappeared into the back again.

Max sipped the coffee. *She's already spiking it. I'll either make it through or be too drunk to care.*

"Next," he called. Warmth and truly southern Southern Comfort spread through his body.

Chapter Five

"Um, Max, do you mind if I go next?"

Max looked up at the timid middle-aged man standing in front of him. Barry Flinn stood in his usual pose with his left upper arm grasped firmly in his right hand with eyes not quite making contact. *He would be so much more attractive if he just had some self-esteem.*

Barry actually looked Max in the eye for the briefest of moments before staring back down at the table. He shifted his weight from one foot to the other. His glasses slid to the end of his nose in their never-ending struggle with gravity, and he eased them back into place with a slightly trembling hand.

"Hi, Barry. Have a seat. I'm glad you came tonight." Max realized his voice had automatically taken on the softer tone he always used when speaking to the owner of Biscuit Acres doggy day care. "How are Sugar and Num-Num doing?"

The slightly balding man's eyes lit up at the mention of his two Chihuahuas. "Oh, they're just fine. They're in the store. You should come say hello when we finish tonight."

"I'd like that," Max said. If there was any way to get Barry to come out of his shell, it was by talking about dogs. Any dogs would do, but mentioning his babies always got the best response. "So what have you got for me?"

Barry slid his folder across the table, blushing involuntarily. "So, um, are you still thinking about getting a dog? It would be good company. Especially now that—" The words—and very nearly Barry, Max was sure—died suddenly.

"It's okay. I know you didn't mean it the way it was sounding," Max assured.

It didn't seem to have any effect. Barry nodded slightly and buried his face in his hands. He refused to look up or speak for the remainder of his time with Max. When told he would receive an email with the FastSheet for his files, Barry whispered, "Thank you," and left immediately.

I guess I'll see the dogs some other time.

Kandy placed Max's food on the table. "Where's Barry? I have his tuna melt."

"He left because he embarrassed himself...again." Max exhaled sharply. "I don't know how he manages to get through life. I've seen mice be less timid." *Well, that sounded worse than I intended.*

"I'll take it to him. He probably just went to get his babies. I'll be right back." She hurried out the door, leaving Max feeling like a jerk.

I didn't say this stuff out loud before Bobby ended things. Did I? I've got to stop before I say something I can't take back. He bit into the Panini and groaned appreciatively.

"Well, there's a sound I haven't heard in a while. You need some time alone? I'm sure we could all leave." The raucous laughter and knee slap that followed the crude comment drew every eye in the room to Jamie Robertson.

"Stop it," his wife, Elaine, hissed. "Do you always have to say the absolute stupidest things that come to your mind?"

"Oh, lay off, woman. He knows I don't have a problem with him being a gay boy." Jamie dropped into the seat next to Max and clapped him on the shoulder.

"Hi, guys. Elaine, you look lovely. Is that a new haircut?" He let Jamie's comments pass as quickly as possible.

She shot daggers at Jamie. "Not that anyone else has noticed. And thank you," she added as an afterthought.

"Hey, I have a new joke for you," Jamie said. "How many gay guys can you fit on a—"

"Heard it," Max said, cutting off the remainder of the oldest joke he knew. "How's business been treating you?"

Without missing a beat, Jamie said, "We can't complain. Best decision we ever made. Vaping is the trend of the future. The Vapor Trail is our Sutter's Mill for the 21st century." He slapped Max's shoulder again. "You should give it a try. Don't need to be quitting smoking to enjoy it and look cool."

"No, thanks." Max rubbed his shoulder and attempted to move farther from the friendly assault. He shuffled through several invoices before coming to a handwritten receipt.

"This says it's for miscellaneous expenses," Max said. He held the paper out for the Robertsons to see. "Do you want me to put it under any specific expense listing?"

"Miscellaneous covers it," Jamie said.

Both men looked at Elaine, who had mumbled something under her breath. "It's just a business expense. Nothing to worry your pretty little head about," Jamie said.

Max noticed the man was looking at him when he spoke, but he knew the words had been intended for Elaine. "So, um, not to beat a dead horse, but five thousand dollars seems like a pretty high amount to just label generically. You might have problems at tax time if you aren't more specific."

"It's a one-time thing. No use getting Uncle Sam's nose poking into something that isn't his business. I'll make that money up in no time." Jamie vaguely gestured at the laptop. "You wave your wand and make those numbers do their little dance. See if I'm not right."

Max took a bite of sandwich to stop himself from commenting on the potential jibe of waving a wand. *Maybe he thinks I'm one of Henny's fairies.*

The bell on the door rang, heralding Kandy's return. On her way past the table with an empty plate, she apologized to Elaine and promised her chai tea latte would be ready in a few minutes.

If anyone works magic, it's Kandy. She keeps all of us content. And maybe just a little fatter. He looked down at his stomach. *Better start hitting the machines again. Can't have a gym owner looking like the Dough Boy.*

"You 'bout finished with that yet? The missus and I have to get to her folks' house. All those dollars shouldn't take too long to add up in the black." Jamie laughed again.

That wasn't even funny. "Well, the numbers are black, but just barely. The five grand took a big chunk out of this month's revenue. I'd try to avoid that next month if you can," Max said.

"That's not going to be a problem," Elaine assured matter-of-factly. She glared at Jamie, but he decided to look at a menu on the wall and missed it.

Max saved the FastSheet and attached it to an email to send to the Robertsons. "That does it. You guys enjoy your evening."

"You, too, and you be sure to let us know if you need any help with your situation," Jamie said. "It's a terrible thing that happened to Skylar. He seemed like a decent enough guy, even if he was a druggie. If you see Bobby, tell him we said hello." He slapped Max on the shoulder one more time.

"Good night, Max," Elaine said. She looked down at the scarf. "That's lovely. Michael Kors?"

"Yes," Max said, beaming. "Who else?"

Elaine ran her hand over it and smiled. "Thanks for everything." She walked to the counter and asked Kandy to get her drink to go.

And now for Eden. God, give me strength.

As if summoned by the mere thought of her name, Eden glided past Max's table, dragging a delicate hand along his arm. She took up position behind him, grasped his head in her hands, and slowly massaged his temples.

"That aura is very dark tonight. We can't have our favorite accountant walking around in the middle of a black hole." Her lilting, sing-song voice managed to soothe and grate on his nerves at the same time. She started rubbing the center of his forehead. "Open that chakra. Let's unclutter that mind and focus on the future."

He could feel her swaying back and forth behind him, and he felt utterly ridiculous. "The only thing I need to open right now is my bladder. Excuse me." He swiveled and stood up, banging his knee against the table. Suppressing far too many curse words, he rushed to the restroom.

Chapter Six

"Max, are you okay?" Kandy asked from the barely-opened door.

"I'm fine, and alone, if you want to come in." He wiped water from his face with a rough, brown paper towel and tossed it into the waste can.

"Eden's waiting for you," she said.

The playful smirk on her face caused him to shake his head, and he mimicked choking her. They laughed. He stared at himself in the mirror and exhaled loudly.

"I think I may be overdoing it tonight. First Bobby, then Skylar, and now the circus—it's all so much to handle at once." His reflection frowned back at him, and he was thankful it didn't do more than that.

"You just have to get through Eden, and then it's over for another month." She stepped up beside him and bumped his leg with her hip. "Have I told you I'm glad you're back? Just wasn't the same without you being here."

He hugged her and cherished the contact with someone who had become a dear friend. "You always say the right thing just when I need it. Thank you."

"It's what I do. Well, that and serving enough caffeine to kill an elephant." She winked at him in the mirror. "Come on, Super Accountant; let's get you out there to tackle the big, bad beast that is Eden's finances."

He nodded and followed her out of the restroom. She moved off to respond to a request from the Gallowyldes, and he plastered another smile on his face and sat down across from Eden.

"I'm so sorry. You know how it is when you've had so much coffee." He had no doubt that Eden would not be bothered by his hasty departure. She hardly ever seemed to be aware of anything beyond the moment. "It's good to see you again. I love your scarf, by the way."

"Oh, why thank you." She looked down, and Max thought she looked surprised by the gold and green silk wound around her neck, as if she was seeing it for the first time. "I believe it was gift from my late husband. He always did love giving me beautiful things."

Max heard the sadness and melancholy in her voice. "I'm sorry. I didn't mean to upset you."

"Oh, you didn't, dear. My darling Winston loved me and instilled in me a joy of beauty. It's why I do what I do." She handed him a thick manila envelope overflowing with paper. "I can't say he did the same thing for numbers."

Max suppressed a sigh. "We'll make it work. We always do." *I don't know how, but we do.* He pulled out a stack of papers and laid them on the table before fishing out a crumpled wad of receipts at the bottom of the envelope.

His sigh was thankfully overshadowed by a deep humming sound. Looking up, he saw Eden holding a large purple crystal in her hands. Her eyes were shut. He hoped she was channeling energy into him to get through the mess she had surely presented.

"Do you think Bobby will be back with us soon?" Eden asked.

Her suddenly asking the question, interrupting her apparent meditation, surprised Max. "I hope he'll be at the gym tomorrow, but I haven't heard from him since he left with the police. Nobody in their right mind thinks he did it."

"Do the police have a different suspect in mind?" she asked.

"They've questioned Corey and me, but other than that, their focus is on Bobby. I guess that makes sense," he conceded. "The boyfriend's always the suspect."

"Is that how you see them, as boyfriends?" Eden's eyes remained closed, but he could still feel them boring into the darkest reaches of his minds. Her knack of shining light in the shadows became maddening at times.

Like now.

Max dropped his pencil and rubbed the bridge of his nose. He didn't want to get into this, but he knew once Eden had started down a path, she didn't stop until she reached her destination.

"What else am I supposed to think?" he asked. "Bobby dumped me and went straight for Skylar. I'm starting to wonder if they weren't doing something before he ended our relationship." He stopped. *That's what's getting me most about this. I don't know for sure. This sucks.*

"If I tell you something, will you promise not to be mad at me?" Eden reverently placed the crystal into a black velvet bag and stared him directly in the eye. "Your aura just got darker," she said with a gentle lilt.

He bit off the angry retort before it left his tongue. Instead, he said, "I'll do my best. No promises."

She nodded, apparently satisfied that was all he was willing to concede. "Skylar wasn't in the picture before the break-up, but he was right after. If you ask me, it wasn't about love."

"Eden, I can't do this. Not right now. I hope you understand." He kept his tone even and fought against tears collecting in his eyes. "I need to focus on this."

He looked down and buried himself in the papers. Part of him felt better knowing Bobby hadn't replaced him before they split. An even bigger part hated knowing that Skylar—*of all people!*—had been the rebound.

Why couldn't it have been someone else? Corey *would have been better. Not less painful, but at least I can see that being more plausible.* A small circle of wetness appeared on the paper he was staring at. *And now I'm crying. This is just great.*

"Your chakras are cleansing themselves," Eden said. Max had never seen her look happier. "Let it all out. Let it flow from you and wash your spirit clean."

"Eden." He said her name and stopped himself—again—to take another deep breath. It honestly did feel good to cry, but doing it in front of her, letting her think it was her success, was not what he wanted.

"I appreciate what you're trying to do for me. Truly, I do," he said. He wiped away the last few stray tears and smiled—genuinely this time. "This just isn't the time or place."

She looked around the room, and Max did the same. Most everyone had left, except the Gallowyldes—who were finishing the last of their preparations to depart—and obviously Kandy. Eden looked back at him, and he had never seen her be so serious in the entire time he had known her.

"You take my papers home and do them later," she ordered. "I'm in no rush, and we both know my business will not become a financial ruin in a couple days. It's survived me this long, and I have zero doubts it will continue to survive in spite of me."

She leaned across the table and took both his hands in hers and forced him to look at her. "You have a lot you're dealing with right now, and I will do everything I can to help you. I'm here for you, you know that, right?"

"I do," he said. "And believe me, I appreciate it." He stuffed her paperwork back into the envelope. "I'll work on this tomorrow and send you the FastSheet on Monday when I get to the gym."

"I don't know why you bother with that," she said, waving away his proposal. "I just delete those and count on the fact that you take care of everything for me. I know. I know." She cut off his usual verbal tirade before he could even open his mouth. "Like I said, it'll survive in spite of me."

She stood up and pulled on her coat. "Come see me on Monday. I want to discuss some things with you. Yes, it's more of my mumbo-jumbo, but it's better than doing nothing—or binge drinking for two months in Barbados."

"Yeah, yeah." He smiled ruefully. "I'll be there. I promise. I just can't promise to drink the Kool-Aid."

"Deal." She pulled him up from his chair and hugged him. "Take care, Max."

"You too." He slumped back into the chair and finished putting everything into the envelope she had given him.

"Do you need anything else, hun?" Kandy asked.

"No, thanks. I'm just finishing up. Do you need me to help you with anything before I go?" he asked.

"Nope." She waved at the Gallowyldes on their way out the door. "You go home and rest. I'll see you on Monday. Or, you could come in for Sunday brunch, if you want."

"Unless I get called to come help at the gym, I think I'm just going to be lazy at home, but I appreciate the offer," he said. She went to finish some work behind the counter, and he shoved everything into his bag.

Back into the cold, he thought miserably. He stood, pulled on his hat and gloves, and wound the scarf around his neck. Wishing Kandy a good night, he went to pick up his bag when he saw a piece of paper lying on the floor.

He bent down, picked it up, and smoothed it out. It was a receipt from Garden of Eden that had obviously fallen out of her gigantic mess. Opening his bag, he went to shove it into the envelope. Something caught his eye right before it left his grip.

The receipt was for a dozen roses—nothing out of the ordinary. However, Eden had written at the bottom what the attached card was supposed to have said:

S—Thanks for a wonderful time. Love, Corey.

Chapter Seven

Max stared at the computer monitor in his office without seeing what was on it. His mind raced with all the possible outcomes from confronting Corey about the receipt from Garden of Eden. All day Sunday he had wrestled with himself, waffling between calling Corey at home or waiting until Monday to speak with him in person.

Something tells me there will be more screaming than speaking, he thought. *After everything we've done for him, this is how he repays Bobby—sleeping with his new boyfriend? I guess I shouldn't be surprised. This* is *Corey I'm talking about, after all.*

When they had first met Corey, he was barely dragging himself in for an interview. They had just opened the gym, and Corey had been recommended by a friend of a friend who thought the young man would be perfect for the job.

The first thought Max had when seeing the disheveled, hungover mess pretending to be a human being was, *No way in hell.* Bobby, though, had seen a wounded little puppy dog that needed to be rescued and tended to. As soon as the extremely short interview ended, Bobby had already made up his mind. No amount of arguing on Max's part would sway him in his decision.

That's classic Bobby. How do I attract these people in my life? I'm responsible. I'm level-headed and intelligent. Why can't I just separate myself from all these...needy people?

"Max, are you in there?" The musical tones of Eden's voice almost sent him under his desk.

He sighed. "Yes." *She's not wasting any time getting started with the torture.* He powered off the monitor and turned, standing up just as Eden walked in. She had obviously been intending to grab his shoulders—like she always did—because her hands slammed into his chest.

"Oh, sorry," she said, apparently confused that he had moved. "Well, I see two months of drinking didn't do anything to destroy your physique."

Max blushed. "Um, thanks. So…"

"Sit down, dear. Relax. That aura of yours is going to explode, and I can't handle that blast of negative energy." She pushed him back into the chair and swiveled him around.

Eden sat a massive cloth bag imprinted with the third eye onto the desk and pulled out various items. She set a purple candle in front of him, lit it, and then wafted her hand above the flame toward his face. A softly hummed tune turned into soothing music emanating from a small, old-style tape player. Her fingers danced along the muscles of his neck before pressing up into the base of his skull in small circular movements.

"Eden, I really appreciate what you're trying to do." He tried to shrug out of her grasp, but she latched onto him like an eagle to a salmon.

"Do. Not. Move." She released her grip when he relaxed into the chair. "Much better. Now, focus on the flame. There is nothing but the flame. Feel the heat penetrate your eyes, your mind, and your spirit. Release your anger and frustration. I said focus!" she snapped when Max groaned.

Relax, or else! He suppressed a chuckle. *Fine.*

He pretended to focus on the flickering orange-red flame dancing gently atop the lavender-scented candle. Maybe if he forced himself to relax, it would get Eden out that much sooner. She hummed along with the music and alternated between rubbing his forehead and his heart.

"Breathe and concentrate, Max." She whispered and hummed close to his ear. "Have you heard from Bobby yet?"

He closed his eyes, losing himself in the feel of her fingers. "After my millionth 'Where the hell are you?' message, he called me at four this morning and said he was leaving town."

"What? Why would he do that?" Eden asked.

"Because he's scared," Max said. He exhaled slowly, not wanting to admit that Eden's gentle touch had eased most of the tension he'd been holding for the past two months. "The police were apparently hammering him pretty badly until the lawyer got there. After he went home, he decided it was better to leave town. Why are the hot ones always so stupid?" he murmured.

"He's not stupid; he's just scared, like you said." Eden ran her fingers through Max's hair from his neck to his forehead and then back again before pushing him slightly forward in the chair. Her palms moved in slow circles over his shoulder blades, and she smiled when he sighed softly.

"I need to prove he didn't kill Skylar," he said. "Crap, that reminds me. I should probably tell Willie, um, Detective Harris about Bobby skipping town. No sense in getting myself into trouble, too."

He heard paper rustling on his desk and glanced to his right without moving his head. Eden groaned as the receipt for Corey's roses fluttered back onto the pile of papers.

"I'm sorry you saw that," she said. "I meant to remove it before you went through everything."

"Do you think Bobby knows?" he asked.

"I'm not certain," she said. "Corey made the order on a day when I was out, and my part-time helper took the order. I didn't know about it until much later."

"I have to talk to Corey about it."

"Why?" Her fingernails dug into the flesh of his face—he hoped unintentionally. "Nothing good will come from that conversation. And if the police find out, it could prove motive for Bobby. A man finds out his new boyfriend is sleeping with someone else—that just screams reason for murder. You won't be doing him any favors."

"Is *this* why you came today?" His words dripped with accusation, and he didn't care.

Her fingers stopped moving briefly. "Honestly, yes. I hate the thought that my negligence may have cast doubt on Bobby, shows what a little twit Corey is…and that you may have been hurt in the process." She rested her right hand above his heart. "You've been damaged enough."

Max looked down at her hand and placed his own atop it. "You're too sweet, Eden, but I can take care of myself."

"No, you can't." She sounded sad. "You want us to believe it, but nobody does."

"What?" He clamped his mouth shut, hating that he had sounded so hurt and angry. "So I'm a source of gossip for everyone in the mall? Well, that's just great!"

"You're supposed to be relaxing, not being an overly dramatic queen." She chuckled when he turned his head enough for her to see his scowl. "I knew that would shut you up, and you know I didn't mean it badly. None of us do, Max. We love you. God knows you've kept most of us in business with your accounting help.

"And we don't pity you or gossip about you. We *worry* about you. There's a very big difference." She moved her hands back to his shoulders. "You take so much on yourself, and we let you. But I think you need to start changing that. This situation with Corey would be a good place to start."

"Do you think Corey killed Skylar? He has motive, too." Max titled his head back and looked up at her. "And while we're on the subject, did you kill Skylar?"

Eden laughed. "I've been guilty of many things, but believe me, murder is not one of them. As for Corey, we're all capable of many things we wish we weren't. I guess that obviously includes me, too, and probably casts doubt on my former protestation of innocence. Oh well. Corey is a lover, not a killer. He's too interested in the next conquest to worry over someone he's conquered. It's not him, if you ask me."

"But there is so much to cast doubt on his innocence," Max protested.

"According to whom? What have you found?" she asked.

Max didn't know what to say. *It's all guesses and anger,* he conceded to himself. *But there is definitely something going on that he doesn't want me to know about. Why else would he be digging through Skylar's locker? And if he wasn't concerned about Skylar, why send him roses?*

"Hey, Max, have you—" Corey burst into the office but cut himself off when he saw Eden. "Oh, I'm sorry. I didn't realize you were busy. Hi, Eden."

"Hi. It's okay. We're finished." She blew out the candle, stopped the music, replaced her items in her purse, and swept from the office like a gentle summer breeze without saying goodbye.

"What's up, Corey?" Max asked. He started wrestling within himself again.

"I, um, lost a vaping device, and I was wondering if you've seen it?"

"Yes." Max stood up and pushed his hand into his pocket, realizing for the first time that it wasn't there. "Oh, I must have left it at Mind Your Own Beans Saturday night. I'll see if Kandy has it."

"Great. I really need it."

"I thought you had two of them," Max said.

Corey stopped in mid-turn on his way out of the office. "Um, yeah, I do, but, that one is, you know, special." Without another word, he left the office.

Oh, you're not getting out of it that easily. Max had made up his mind, and Corey wasn't going to like it.

Chapter Eight

Corey was making a hasty retreat. He had made it past the entrance to the juice bar before Max caught up with him. Max quickly looked around, glad to see no one else in the room. No prying eyes.

"Corey, we need to talk," he said.

Corey looked over his shoulder but continued walking. "What's up?"

Max lunged forward, grabbed Corey by the arm, and ushered him into the small storage room at the back. "We need to talk *privately.*"

"Ow. Okay, but can you please let go? You're hurting me," Corey whined.

Max released his grip and looked at the five red marks he had left behind. "I'm sorry. We just have to settle something."

To Max, Corey looked surprised and worried rolled up into one big ball of nervous tension. "Talk? About what? We talked the other night."

Max closed the door behind him after turning on the light. "Oh, you talked, alright, but it was just to ease my mind and throw me off your trail."

"What? Who even talks like that?" Corey asked. He leaned against a wire rack holding bottles of juice and packages of various powders. His obvious attempt to appear casual wasn't fooling anyone.

"Just drop it." Max thrust the receipt at Corey. "I know about you and Skylar. My God! How could you do that?"

"You're crazy. I wasn't doing anything!" Corey shouted. "Besides, it's none of your business what I do with my personal life."

"No, but it *is* my business when you start bringing it to work, and when it starts affecting everyone here. Oh, and it's also my business when someone gets killed in my gym!" Max shouted back. "Did you kill Skylar?"

Corey stared at him. "I am telling you for the last time, Max, I did *not* kill Skylar. I loved him." His teeth slammed together. "I loved him," he whispered.

Max didn't know what to say. Corey had completely derailed his train of thought. When the words had time to sink in, he said, "Wow, I never thought I would say this, but I believe you."

Corey scowled. "I know what you and everyone else think about me, but I'm capable of being more than just a toy. I cared about Bobby, and I didn't want to hurt him, but I loved Skylar." He looked pointedly at Max. "*And I did not kill him.*"

"Then why were you going through his locker after Harris and the police left?" Max asked.

Corey sighed. "I don't want to tell you. You'll be mad."

"What do you think I am right now?" Max snapped.

"Okay. God!" Corey held his hands up in surrender. "I had to make sure they didn't find his stash."

"Drugs? He had drugs in his locker? What about Bobby trying to get him clean?" Max asked. *I can't believe this!*

Corey looked down at the floor. "He obviously didn't want to quit, but he didn't want Bobby to know. Not because he was using Bobby or anything. He just liked the attention. You know better than anyone that Bobby isn't hard on the eyes."

Max growled and watched Corey sink closer to the floor. "I honestly don't expect much out of you, but I will admit that I expected more than this. You do realize that I have to tell Detective Harris about this, don't you? If I don't, I could get into trouble, too."

"You can't do that. They'll think I—"

"Yes, they'll think you had motive. Just like I do," Max said. "It seems pretty cut and dry to me."

"But it's not," Corey said. "I swear. It was just sex and drugs. I didn't kill him. How many times do I have to say it?"

Max shook his head. *Bobby is going to be devastated. I'm not going to be the one to tell him. Let Corey squirm through all that like the little snake he is.*

"I really need the device back, too," Corey said.

"What's so special about that thing anyway?" Max demanded.

Corey sighed. "We found a way to modify it to smoke pot."

"What? How?" Max stared at him. *This just gets worse and weirder with every word out of his mouth.*

"It doesn't matter. I just need it back. Please. I don't want it hurting Skylar or Bobby."

"Or you," Max said. "That's what this is really about."

"Fine," Corey said. "I don't want it hurting me, either. Happy? And please, don't tell the cops about this."

"Did Jamie help you alter the e-cig?"

"No," Corey said. The look on his face convinced Max he was telling the truth. "Skylar came up with the process on his own. He was planning to start selling the stuff to his friends, and I was going to be his partner."

"In more than one sense of the word, huh?" Max said.

"Stop! I get it! I'm a piece of crap. Tell the world. I'll call my parents, and you can tell them. Okay?" Corey leaned his head against the metal support of the rack.

Max pulled his cell phone from his pocket and dialed Kandy's number. He asked if she had seen the device he left on the table Saturday night, hoping not to have to explain why he was asking.

"Ok, thanks. I appreciate you." He nodded needlessly. "Yeah, I'll come by for lunch. Thanks. Love you too. Bye."

He ended the call and stared at Corey. "Well, we're out of luck. Kandy said she never saw it."

"So you lost it?" Corey asked.

"Hey, don't put this on me." Max bit off the rest of his verbal tirade as a thought occurred to him.

What if someone knew what it was and took it?

Chapter Nine

Mind Your Own Beans just finished the lunch rush when Max walked in shortly after one o'clock. He had passed Henrietta on the sidewalk out front and rushed back to open the door to Crumbles because her hands were full. She thanked him and invited him to stop by for some fresh pumpkin cookies when he finished his lunch date with Kandy.

"Oh, you're a savior in disguise," Max said, almost throwing himself into the chair across from Kandy. The tuna melt smelled amazing, and she had obviously gone out of her way to save a bowl of her homemade tomato soup. This made up for the morning.

Well, almost.

"I'm sorry about the vaping device. I didn't even know you had one," she said.

"I don't. It belongs to Corey…well, Skylar." He bit into the sandwich and sighed appreciatively. "Marry me."

She laughed over the cup of coffee in her hands. "I think we've had that discussion more times than I'm comfortable with, dear."

"Mm-hmm," he mumbled. He washed down the bite with a sip of coffee and looked up at Detective Harris walking through the door.

When Kandy saw the smile on his face, she turned around. "Hello, Detective. Would you like a cup of coffee?"

"If it's no trouble," he said, sitting beside Max.

"It's a coffee shop. If getting coffee is a problem, I'm in the wrong business," she said with a smile. "How about something to eat?"

Harris looked at the food sitting in front of Max. "Sure. I could go for a garden salad without dressing."

"Mr. Healthy now?" Max asked after Kandy disappeared.

"I just do it to offset the ungodly amount of donuts I eat. I don't want to go from gawky to doughy in less than ten years." Harris patted his stomach.

Without thinking, Max reached out and patted it, too. "Wow. I don't think you have to worry about that. Those abs should be registered as deadly weapons."

Harris blushed. "Thanks. You know, being around you is doing wonders for my ego. I just need to be careful, or I won't be able to fit my head through the door on the way out."

"If that happens, I'll put you to work washing dishes," Kandy said. She set a bowl in front of Harris and handed him his coffee before resuming her seat. "I could use a good bus boy, too, so you may want to be careful."

"Can't be any worse than what I do now," Harris said before taking a drink. "So, Max, have you heard from Bobby today? He's not answering his phone, and I thought he might be at the gym."

"He, um…" Max cleared his throat and coughed into his hand. "He's, um, gone.

"*What?*" Harris's coffee sloshed onto his hand and the table when he slammed his cup down. He cursed and flung the hot liquid onto the floor.

Kandy wiped up the mess. "I'll leave you two alone. Let me know if you need anything." She quickly disappeared.

"He's gone. Left town." Max could feel Harris staring at him, but he couldn't find the courage to look back.

"When?" The harsh tone of Harris's voice could shatter granite.

"This morning. *Early* this morning." Max tore the crust off of his sandwich and dropped it onto the plate.

"And you're just now telling me?" Harris slammed his napkin onto the table, stood up, and immediately sat back down. He leaned toward Max, invading personal space in the way only a cop can. "Look at me. I *said* look—at—me."

Slowly, reluctantly, Max forced himself to look into Harris's eyes.

"He's my prime suspect, and his leaving town pretty much convinces me he killed Skylar Pratt. Regardless of what you say," Harris said. "And the fact that you didn't tell me means I could charge you with several things, too." He leaned back and crossed his arms over his chest. "I trusted you, Max. I trusted you, and this is my reward."

"I'm sorry," Max whispered. He knew better than to look away.

"I know that we haven't seen each other in a while, but I thought you were my friend," Harris said. "Is this how you treat your friends? How you repay their trust in you?"

"Bobby's my friend, too." Max leaned back, mimicking Harris's posture. "I promise I meant to tell you. I just had a lot of things come up, and it slipped my mind. Honestly. I'm not covering for Bobby."

"I was afraid he might flee, but I didn't have enough evidence to arrest him," Harris said. "Well, his personal bank account will be frozen. I assume he has access to the gym's account as well."

"Yes."

"Well, you might want to get as much money as you can, because it'll probably be frozen, too," Harris said.

Max stared. *No amount of food can salvage this day now. How did we get to this point? Would telling him about Corey and Skylar make the situation better or worse? I wish I knew what to do!*

"I can't believe you'd jeopardize yourself and your future for someone who may have killed his boyfriend," Harris said.

"I've known Bobby long enough to know he didn't do this. I just can't prove it. Yet," Max added forcefully.

"I shouldn't do this, but I'll keep your…omission between us," Harris said. "Just don't do something *else* stupid. Okay?" He leaned forward and obviously pressed a smile onto his lips.

"I think stupid is my middle name sometimes," Max said. "William, I swear, Bobby didn't do it. I don't know who did, but I know in my heart of hearts that it's not him."

"So you keep saying, and I believe that you believe that," Harris said. "I just don't have the luxury. That doesn't mean I'm giving up and treating this like an open-and-shut case. I'm still looking at evidence and questioning anyone I can think of. Do you have anything else that could help me with that?"

Max opened his mouth and quickly shut it. *I do,* he screamed silently, *but I don't know if I should tell you.*

"Excuse me, ladies." The comment was followed by a laugh and a knee slap that sent Max's blood pressure through the roof.

Harris was instantly on his feet, staring Jamie Robertson in the eye with a look that could have frozen mercury on the sun. "It's *Detective* Harris, and I can assure you I am no lady. Now, if you don't mind, I'm in the middle of police business, but if you want to continue to be an ass, I can arrest you for impeding an officer in his duties. Questions?"

Jamie turned white, and Max turned his head to hide his wide smile. *I wish I had a video of that. Priceless!*

"Um, I'm sorry, Detective. I didn't mean anything by it. Ask Max. He knows I like to josh around with him." He looked at Max with the desperate look of a mouse cornered by a cat. "Right, Max? Buddy?"

Max hesitated long enough to enjoy Jamie's pain before saying, "It's okay, William."

Harris remained standing and crossed his arms over his chest. "Did you need something, Mr. Robertson?"

"Yes, I did. I do. Can we talk somewhere else?" Jamie asked.

Harris pointed at the door and followed the man outside. Max ate the rest of his sandwich while he watched them talking. Jamie went from mouse to animated puppet. When their conversation was obviously over, he glanced at Max through the glass of the door, and then turned, all but running away.

"What was that all about?" Max asked when Harris came back in.

The detective took a long drink of coffee. "Is Corey Barnes at work today? I have some questions for him."

Chapter Ten

"Have another cookie, Max." Henrietta pushed the plate closer to him and smiled the devilish smile that sent him into flashbacks of his childhood and being twenty pounds overweight.

"Believe me, three is more than enough," he said.

"Oh, nonsense. You own a gym for goodness sake. Just run on the treadmill or lift those silly weights like you do," she chided gently. "You need the pick-me-up. Don't try denying it. My darlings told me about that business with Corey."

Max stared at her. She was stirring her hot tea and humming some tune she said reminded the fairies of home. *She hasn't a care in the world, and knows far more than anyone has a right to.*

"What do you mean?" he asked.

"Oh, you know, dear. Him, Skylar, and that sordid business with the…" Her voice trailed off as she cocked her head to the side and her eyes lost focus. After a few seconds of silence, she said, "Well, let's just say you know what I'm talking about."

She picked up an empty saucer from the floor, stirred some honey and sugar together in the center, and then put it back. "There you go, darlings," she whispered.

"Henny, who have you been talking to about *that*?" He scrutinized her face for any reaction that would betray her. *Betray her how? It's not like I'm in her head and know what she's thinking. God, she probably* does *talk to fairies, and she's the only one smart enough to hear them.*

She sighed, clearly exasperated, and pushed the plate of cookies closer. It bumped into his arm. "Max, you're just like my John. You never listen when I tell you anything. It's my darlings.

I've asked them to watch over you and help you through this nasty business. They heard you talking about that stuff. I'm just offering a kind ear."

He considered his next words carefully. At least, he hoped he did. Henny could be very touchy when it came to her darlings, and even the wrong syllable of a word given more or less emphasis than it warranted could cause her to clam up or become hurt.

"Do you know something I don't? Please, even the littlest piece of information could help. Especially since Bobby's left town and made himself look even guiltier," he said.

"I know, dear." She shook her head and clucked her tongue. "This whole thing is a mess that won't easily be cleaned up." She picked up a cookie and broke off a piece. She popped it into her mouth and placed the remainder on the saucer on the floor. "I wish I could help you with money, Max, but you know our books. There is no possible way we could do it without getting ourselves into financial trouble."

"Don't you worry about that," he said and patted her hand reassuringly. "I'll take care of myself. I don't want you and John to do something you can't or shouldn't. It's enough knowing you want to. That's what counts."

"We're always here, dear, and my darlings have agreed to watch over Bobby. Did I already tell you that? I think I did." She cocked her head to the side and mentally slipped away again. "You haven't eaten that yet?"

She and Max looked at a cookie he didn't remember picking up. He emulated her earlier actions of splitting the cookie between him and the fairies, but the saucer beneath her chair was empty.

"Um, Henny…"

"Yes."

"Do you have a cat?"

"Oh, no, dear! My darlings don't like them. Cats just scare the dickens out of them." She looked down at the empty saucer and smiled. "They do love the pumpkin cookies. Would you like a dozen to take with you?"

He nodded absentmindedly and mumbled thanks. She walked a few feet to the counter, picked up a pink box tied with an ornate white bow, and set it on the table in front of him.

"Share a few with Corey. He's going to need them now that that handsome detective of yours has finished with him." She patted him on the shoulder and walked away, humming her little song.

The door chimed, and Max looked up.

Detective Harris walked in, blowing into his obviously cold hands in an attempt to warm them up.

"As long as I've known her, it still freaks me out," Max muttered. "I wish I knew how she does it." He looked over his shoulder and then back at Harris. "Cookie?" he asked, shoving the plate across the table.

Chapter Eleven

Harris dropped into the chair Henny had vacated. The scowl on his face made Max want to look away, but he resisted and maintained eye contact. *This isn't going to go well, but I did keep information from him. Again. I didn't really have a chance to tell him before Jamie opened* his *big mouth, but I don't think William is going to see it that way.*

"Anything you need to tell me?" Harris demanded.

Max felt his eyes slipping toward the table and refocused his gaze. "Um, about what?"

"Max. Don't. I've treated you with nothing but respect during this mess, and I don't expect anything less from you," Harris said. "I thought we discussed this, and I'm finished playing nice."

The tone of Harris's voice broke Max's heart. It was heavily tinged with disappointment. Max sighed, closed his eyes, and scrubbed his face with his hands. The smell of pumpkin cookies assaulted his nose.

"I'm sorry. You're right," he said, looking back at Harris. "In my defense, though, I wasn't hiding this from you. I *was* going to tell you. I just didn't know how or when to do it."

"Max." Harris stared at him. There was obviously a war going on in the man's head, and Max didn't know if he was going to welcome the victor or despise it. "I want you to tell me everything you know about Corey and Skylar. When I say everything, I mean exactly that. *Everything!* Got it?"

Max nodded. *God, help me. I'm so afraid this is going to get ugly.*

He plunged into the deep end of the facts as he knew them. Nothing was left unsaid about his conversation with Corey from earlier in the morning. Harris's expression never changed. He didn't take any notes, but Max could tell the detective scrutinized every word, every detail. It was all getting filed away. *William always was an information sponge.*

"Thank you," Harris said when Max finished. "I'm not trying to be a jerk, Max. I've just dealt with too much crap as a cop to be played by someone I...um, a friend."

"I'm sorry I didn't tell you sooner. I swear I really was going to, though," he said. "Jamie just beat me to."

"I believe you." Harris contemplated the last cookie on the plate, shrugged, and bit into it. "Oh my God! Do they put crack in these things? Because I want another one already."

Max laughed. "If Henny hears you say that—if her *darlings*—hear you say that, she'll send you out of here with more cookies than one person can eat in a lifetime."

"And I would probably accept," Harris said around another mouthful. "Who are her darlings?"

"My fairies, dear," Henrietta said from behind the counter. "My darling little fairies. I take care of them, and they take care of me, my bakery, and those people I consider dear friends." She looked pointedly at Max and smiled. "I'll get you two some more cookies. I'm so happy you like them."

"Fairies?" Harris whispered after Henny disappeared into the back of the bakery. "As in little winged creatures that fly around?"

"*Invisible,* too," Max said. "They give her comfort. Well, the thought of them does. It's anyone's guess if they're real or not." If Harris had been wearing glasses, Max realized he would be looking over the top of them at that instant.

"You don't really believe in them, do you?" Harris asked.

Max shrugged. "Either they're real or that woman is the uncanny knower of things unknowable you will ever meet. There are times I wonder if she doesn't have miniature spy cameras stashed in all the stores here. I even search for them sometimes."

"The cameras or the fairies?" Harris asked with a smirk.

"Both," Max said. He laughed. "Hang around her long enough and you'll get spooked by her 'darlings,' too." Max looked around and then leaned closer to Harris across the table. "Can I ask you a question?"

Harris leaned in, too, meeting Max half-way. "You can ask. I can't guarantee an answer though, depending on the question."

"I understand," Max said. "Has the M.E. given any indication when a toxicology report will be completed on Skylar?"

"Oh," Harris said. Max had a feeling that wasn't the question he had been expecting. "Well, it is Oklahoma, and the problems in the State Medical Examiner's office aren't exactly a well-guarded secret." He leaned back in the chair. "I'm still waiting on results from an investigation over a year old. My expectations for this case are not high."

"So, if Bobby gets arrested, he could be sitting in jail for a very long time," Max said.

"That's a given since he fled. There's nothing I can do about it. You know that, right?" Harris asked.

"I do," Max said. He realized he was still leaning expectantly toward Harris and sat back in the chair. "What's going to happen to Corey?"

Harris sighed. "Other than the fact some drug dealer is probably going to put a bullet into his head someday? I don't know. I did have him taken in for more questioning. He'll probably be charged with removing evidence from a crime scene, but I don't know that it will stick because that evidence is now missing."

"Sorry about that," Max mumbled.

"Not your fault," Harris said with a reassuring smile. "It just leads me to think the killer is someone who works at the mall."

"Same," Max said. "I just can't figure out who. Everyone except Daniel Carheart, the insurance man, was at Mind Your Own Beans Saturday night. Anyone of them could have stolen the device. I had it just lying on the table. No clue it was possibly evidence."

"It's okay." Harris patted his hand.

Max looked down and smiled.

"What?" Harris asked, clearly confused.

"Anything you want to ask me?" he asked.

Harris blushed. "Not right now. Not with you being part of an investigation." He took a deep breath and held it a while before blowing it out. "However...when this mess is over, I wouldn't mind asking you a question."

"I wouldn't mind answering a question." Max laughed and shook his head. "My God! William Harris. Who would have ever thought the two of us would ever...well, we'll see, I guess. I just never, ever dreamed it was a possibility."

"That only makes one of us," Harris said, turning red. "I guess I should confess now. I always hoped we would. I was just never your type, I think."

"You were," Max said reassuringly. "You just didn't have the self-esteem to realize it. I'm glad that's changed. Honestly."

Harris cleared his throat. "I have to go back to the office. I'll be in touch. And, please, if you have new information, tell me right away. Okay?"

Max nodded and started to speak, but Henrietta cut him off by inserting another pink box tied with white ribbon in between him and Harris.

"One for the road, Detective." She bent down and retrieved the saucer from the floor, briefly scrutinizing the piece of cookie Max had placed on it earlier. "You have a good day, and just let me know if you need anything. I'm at your disposal. So are my cookies."

"Thank you, Mrs. Gallowylde." Harris tucked the box under his arm and left.

"Oh, dear," Henrietta said, grasping Max's arm. "That man is quite smitten with you."

Max blushed. "I'm sure you and I are both just imaging things."

"If you say so, dear." A timer went off in the back of the kitchen. "Back to work. Don't forget your cookies, and remember I'll have more if you need them."

Max thanked her. He could see Harris pulling out of the parking lot, and thinking of the man caused him to smile. *William Harris. What a small world.*

He picked up the box of cookies on his way to the door. Outside, the freezing wind slammed into his face. *Why did I ever leave Barbados?*

Chapter Twelve

Max pressed the "off" button on the treadmill and walked to a halt. It felt good to run off cookies and frustration, especially at the end of the day when no one else was in the gym. He wiped away a copious amount of sweat on his forehead, draped the towel over his shoulders, and walked toward the locker room.

Corey had returned from the police department after a few hours of talking to Harris's team, and he hadn't been happy. He had started out just scowling at Max through the windows of the main workout area. Then he had built up enough courage to become a whirling dervish of flapping hands and self-righteous tirade.

Max ended it all with a single look that conveyed his *I-don't-care* attitude. "We've been down this road more times than I care to think about. You did it. You're wrong. It's not my fault you can't accept accountability for your own actions. Are we done?"

Corey huffed off, muttering under his breath. Within minutes the sounds of various inanimate objects being slammed down and tossed aside emanated from the juice bar.

Oh well. He'll get over it, and if he doesn't, I will.

In the locker room, Max stripped out of his clothes, leaving a stinking, sweat-stained holocaust of clothing in his wake on the way to the shower. The burst of cold water felt only mildly nerve shattering, but it warmed quickly. His initial thought had been to shower quickly and get back into his office to put the finishing touches on Eden's account, but that thought slowly gave way to lingering in the relaxing fingers of hot water massaging away the remainders of his tension.

I can't believe I thought one day would be enough to get through that gigantic mess of papers and numbers. A super-computer couldn't have done that.

Finally relenting to his sense of duty nagging at him, he turned off the water, flicking droplets from his chest and extremities before retrieving the towel he'd left draped over a bar near the door.

Once dressed, he scooped up his gym clothes and shoved them in a mesh bag. He closed his locker and found himself staring at Skylar's locker. Opening the door, he stared in at the stark emptiness of the gun-metal grey space.

Corey said Skylar hid stuff in here. Maybe he missed something on his hasty retrieval run.

The most likely place to start was a false bottom, which turned out to be exactly the case. Dust and a few stray fibers from cloth of some kind littered the bottom of the small area. Max stuck his head in to examine it from all sides but found nothing noteworthy.

A quick search through the rest of the locker ended nowhere. Skylar had apparently only had the one hiding place. Max closed the door, shaking his head. Slowly, an idea formed in his mind.

He opened his own locker and felt along the bottom. Nothing. The other staff all kept locks on theirs, like he did. Luckily, he knew the combination for Bobby's, and had the door open without any issue.

The police had rummaged through the contents and left the resulting mess for Bobby to clean up later. Max pulled everything out and placed it neatly on a wooden bench in the middle of the aisle.

It took some effort, but he was finally able to pry up the thin plate of metal. *Jackpot!* The small cubbyhole contained a piece of paper—obviously a letter—and a small hard-plastic case. He unfolded the paper and started reading its contents before he realized it was from Bobby to Skylar.

He stopped reading, involuntarily crumpling the paper in his fist. *I can't do this. I shouldn't be doing this. If I go looking for things I don't want to know, I'm going to find them.* He smoothed out the paper, folded it neatly, and slid it into the back pocket of his pants.

The plastic case had a small slide that held it closed. He pushed it back and popped open the lid. Something fell out onto the floor before he could catch it. Bending down he realized it was a syringe.

This looks like what Corey uses for insulin.

The syringe was empty, and the orange safety cap over the needle was still in place. He put it back into the case, next to a small, unmarked glass bottle of clear liquid and a small metal container. It contained marijuana and a slip of paper with extremely tiny handwritten printing on it. He had never seen Skylar's writing before, but he would almost bet this was it.

You no who wants a larger cut. Getting rediculous.

So Corey and Skylar had a third person involved. I bet Bobby didn't even know the little idiot was using his locker as a stash. And from the looks of it, not for a dictionary.

A muffled crash from elsewhere in the gym caused him to jump. *What the hell? I thought Corey went home.*

He closed the case and shoved it into his pocket before replacing the metal plate and cramming everything back into the locker. *I'll organize later.*

He stalked through the door from the locker room into the hallway fully intent on finding Corey and thrashing him. *I am just about at the end of my rope with him. First it's drugs, then it's sleeping with Skylar, and now it's throwing a temper tantrum because he doesn't want to face being an adult. I swear if we didn't need him so badly right now, I would fire him just because.*

He walked down the hall, past the sauna on his right—failing in his attempt not to think about Skylar lying dead on the floor—and the main workout area on his left. Half of the lights in the free weights room were on, and he knew for a fact he had turned all of them off.

He pushed open the door and stuck his head into the room. A small rack of free weights was lying on its side, its contents spread in a small area of the floor.

"Corey, are you in here?" He waited a few seconds before pulling his head back out and glancing down the hallway. The lights to the juice bar were off.

"Corey!" he shouted down the hall. Leaving the door open, he made his way to the front. He grunted in frustration.

Staring out the entryway doors, he saw that Corey's car wasn't in its usual spot. A strange tingling shot up his spine moments before he saw a black blur of movement reflected in the glass.

His attempt to turn and confront the attacker halted midway when something heavy slammed into the side of his head.

Chapter Thirteen

Max opened his eyes and simultaneously put one hand on the side of his head and the other one over his mouth. A muffled moan escaped from him, but luckily nothing from his stomach did.

He felt a third hand on his shoulder and finally saw Harris kneeling above him. "Somebody hit me in the head," he said.

"I know. I am a detective after all." Harris smiled softly, obviously intent to take the worried sting from his words.

"Your timing is off," Max groaned, but he still smiled slightly in spite of the parade marching around the inside of his skull. "Did you see who did it?"

"No. They were long gone by the time I found you," Harris said. When Max tried to sit up, Harris gently restrained him. "No, just stay there, and I'll call an ambulance."

"You take me," Max said. "I can't afford another bill right now. Oh, God. I want to puke so badly."

"Getting hit in the head will do that."

"A doctor and a detective?" Max asked, quirking his eye brow.

"I've also been the recipient of my fair share of concussions. Police work isn't exactly a zero-contact sport, you know." Harris looked over his shoulder through the glass doors.

"Did the person break in, or did Corey forget to lock the door on his way out?" Max asked.

"The door was unlocked when I got here. The safe bet is on Corey, although we don't know that for sure. It could be anyone who has a key to the gym," Harris offered.

"That list has three names on it. Bobby's gone. I didn't hit myself over the head with a small truck, I assure you. So, that leaves Mr. Responsible himself." Max suppressed another urge to throw up and finally remembered the plastic case in his pocket. His hand darted toward it. *Gone. Of course it's gone.*

"What are you doing?" Harris asked.

Max told him about the case and its contents. "Skylar and Corey were apparently dealing with someone else for their drugs."

"Well, *that* list will have more than three names on it. I can promise you that," Harris said. "Looks like Mr. Barnes and I need to have another discussion—a *very* long discussion."

"I'm just glad you don't think Bobby did it," Max said with a smile. He tried to sit up, slowly, but no matter his speed, his head and stomach still wished death upon him.

Harris supported Max's neck and moved around behind him, offering his body for support. "Don't be mad, but part of me still believes he did. That's just the cop in me."

Max leaned against him and resisted the urge to nod. "I'll forgive you, but just this once."

"You may have to forgive that many times over. That's just the nature of who and what I am now," Harris said. "But we have plenty of time to work all those quirks out later."

"You're very sure of yourself," Max said.

"That's part of being a cop, too." He smiled down at Max. "You ready to go the rest of the way?"

"You're moving a little fast, aren't you, Detective?" Max chuckled and instantly regretted ever being born. He groaned.

"And that's what you get," Harris chided. "The rest of the way *to your feet,* Max. We have to do it, unless you let me call an ambulance."

"You could just shoot me and finish the job. That would probably be less painful," Max said.

"You're not going to get that lucky. Now, up we go. I'm right here to help. Take your time."

Got this. Yeah, right! He slowly leaned forward and pulled his knees up to chin. He took a brief rest and then began the rest of the arduous journey. *Finally!*

"See, that wasn't so bad." Harris said.

"For you, maybe," Max scoffed. "I need to get my coat and keys from my office."

They walked—slowly—into the office, and Harris helped Max on with his coat. Max realized he had the FastSheet program running on his computer and had Harris shut it down. Nothing in the office had been touched.

Whoever waylaid me apparently wasn't after money. That just leaves Corey's damn drugs. I am so going to kill him, after I go through this whole place and find every little bit of the stuff he's brought in here.

Harris sorted through the keys on Max's key ring until he found the one for the gym. "Ok, St. Francis is the closest hospital. Is that okay with you?"

"Fine," Max said, taking the offered arm for support as they left the office. "Just as long as this all stops."

"It will—eventually. Now, soldier on."

"Shut up," Max mumbled. His elbow jabbed into Harris ribs, and Max repeated the action when the detective laughed.

Harris turned off the lights and locked the door while offering support to Max. They stepped off the curb on their way to Harris's vehicle. *My God, did he have to park all the way out there.*

"What's that?" Harris asked.

Max looked where he indicated. "My guess is that would be the barbell our mystery guest used to cave in the side of my skull."

"You okay to wait here?" When Max confirmed he would, Harris walked over and used a small piece of cloth from his pocket to pick it up. "Ten pounder. At least it wasn't something bigger," he said as he walked back.

"Yeah. Lucky me," Max grumbled. "Do you think you'll get any prints off that?"

"Lots, I'm sure," Harris confirmed. "Unfortunately, it'll most likely be everyone *but* the assailant. Sorry."

"It's okay. I'm getting used to my luck being nothing but crap. I've got two months' worth of experience with it so far." Max slid into the seat of Harris's Silverado and put on his seat belt.

Harris put the barbell into the back seat of the club cab and then started the truck. With no traffic on the side street, they zipped through the red light, went under I-44, bypassed the next red light to turn left, and were quickly on their way toward Yale Avenue.

"It's a beautiful night," Harris said, "even with the cloud cover."

"And lucky me, I still got to see stars," Max said.

Harris laughed and turned onto Yale, stomping the accelerator to the floor.

Chapter Fourteen

Max's head pounded. He and Harris hadn't left the emergency room until almost four o'clock, and by the time he got home, sleep was the last thing on his throbbing mind. He decided to take the day off and close the gym. By the time he arrived at Tight/Fit, he'd decided to go over every inch of it and find everything anyone had been trying to hide from him.

He called from the warmth of the Jeep and told Corey a pipe had burst due to the cold, overnight temperatures; a plumber would be working most of the day to fix the problem. Almost certain the tone of his voice betrayed his true intentions, Max did his best to sound as normal as possible.

I'm not going to give him a chance to remove all his little stashes. It'll be better if I can find them and confront him all at once. This is it. I'm not going to die just so he can continue to make money. He'll be gone long before that.

He decided to keep the previous night's events a secret from everyone else at the mall and asked Harris to do the same. The attacker had most likely only gone after him because he had been alerted by the falling weights. Otherwise, nothing would have happened.

At least I hope not.

He had side-stepped most of Corey's questions. The biggest ones had been whether Max needed help and if Corey was going to be paid since "It's not my fault I'm missing work."

Max had bit his tongue and told Corey he would be paid, and his help was most definitely not needed. It was just going to be a miserable day filled with using a shop-vac to remove water and avoiding plumber's crack.

True to form, Corey hadn't put up much resistance to the idea. "That'll give me more time at The Toolbox. Thanks, Max. Have fun." The call ended far too cheerfully.

"I'll hit you upside the head with a toolbox," Max had grumbled as he mashed the button to end the call. He grabbed a bottle of pain pills prescribed by the ER doctor, thankful for 24-hour pharmacies, and washed down a little pill with a big gulp of water.

Harris had offered to take the day off work and help with the search. Max had thanked him kindly for it, but ultimately turned him down. He knew the detective was very busy, and his own investigations—not just Skylar's murder, but others, too—were more important than tossing a building in a search for drugs. Besides, Harris had the barbell, and Max really wanted to know if they could get any good prints from it. Not that he held out much hope after what Harris had said.

Max absent-mindedly ran his fingers over the goose egg on his head, wincing at the stabbing pain he summoned forth. The stocking cap he pulled on slid over the same spot, eliciting a shudder and suppressed whimper.

Morning opened up with a good dose of freezing rain which slowly turned into large, fluffy snowflakes around nine o'clock. Max hated days like this. At the first sight of any kind of precipitation, Oklahoma drivers became idiots. Either they drove a hundred miles per hour on ice because they thought 4X4 pickups were God's gift, or they crawled along at five miles per hour because they were too afraid to be on the roads in the first place but felt the calling to be an impediment to everyone else.

Not that I'm bitter about it, he thought on his approach to the front doors. The sidewalk was a treacherous step away from a twisted ankle or a bruised bottom, but Max was able to maneuver along it with the grace of a drunken penguin on a bobbing ice floe. Along the way, when he wasn't watching his feet, he peered through the windows to make sure no unwanted visitors were waiting for him to come in.

The door locked behind him, and he turned on as many lights as he could. His ears strained to pick up the faintest noise, but he heard nothing more than the compressor on the refrigerator in the juice bar kick in after a few minutes of silence.

Releasing a breath he didn't realize he'd been holding, he made his way cautiously to his office and turned on the computer. He hung his coat on the rack in the corner. The computer finished booting, and he pulled up the email.

Of course. He dropped into his chair and fired off a response to Elizabeth Walker, who was very upset that for the second time in two weeks his gym had interrupted her routine. The urge to tell her where she could go died before it reached his fingers, and he offered a simple apology instead—along with a complimentary pass for one of her uppity friends she liked to drag along in the wake of her high-and-mightiness.

Corey Barnes and Elizabeth Walker. God save me from both of them. He pulled up the FastSheet he had finished for Eden the night before and sent it to her. *For all the good it will do. I can't believe she actually told me she doesn't do anything with them. Well, no, I guess I can. It is Eden after all, bless her heart.*

With those tasks settled, he turned off the computer and decided on a plan of attack. It was going to take a while to go through the entire gym. The most likely places, though, would be the juice bar and the locker room. He started with the former.

Corey's little corner of the world looked immaculate, as always. *Why can't his life be this spotless?* He started in the storage room. The shelves contained mostly canisters and small foil pouches. He opened every lid, popped the top off of every box, and rummaged through every square inch of everything else. There were no cubbyholes cut out of the sheet rock or loose floor tiles. It was all perfectly clean.

He went through the kitchen area of the bar, repeating his actions from the store room. In the refrigerator he found several concoctions in sports bottles that Corey had labeled as various juice and powder combinations. Most smelled atrocious, but none of them smelled illegal. None of the containers had false bottoms.

In the little compartment for butter, he found two clear glass bottles. One had a prescription label, marking it as Corey's insulin, and the other, the exact same size, had no label. He picked them up and inspected them, remembering the syringe and bottle from the stolen plastic case. The bottles looked similar.

Max pulled his cellphone out of his pocket and dialed Corey, already hating himself for what he was about to do. "Hey, it's me. Do you have more insulin at home?

"What do you mean by more?" Corey asked.

"Well, I was trying to get a drink out of the refrigerator, and the two bottles you had stored in the door fell out and shattered," Max said. "I'm really sorry. I know this stuff is expensive. I'll pay for more."

"Oh, that. Yeah, don't worry about it, sweetie. That was old stuff that I needed to throw away. Are you okay? You didn't get cut, did you?"

"No, I'm good. Just worried I was going to get you into trouble," Max told him.

Corey laughed. *"Well, that would be a first time the shoe was on the other foot, huh?"*

"Yeah," Max growled. "Glad you're set. Talk to you later. Bye."

He grabbed a storage bag from a cabinet, slipped the bottles inside, and called Harris to ask him if the lab at the police department could run some tests on what he'd found.

"Max, you do realize that if you found something illegal, I can't use it unless we can clearly link it back to Corey, right?" Harris asked. *"And even then there's no guarantee a judge will accept it."*

"I know. I'm not doing this to get Corey into trouble. I just need to put a stop to it, and maybe it'll get me closer to who his other partner was." Max bit his lip. "That person is most likely the one who killed Skylar. I just want to end this."

"You doing this on your own may end it in a bad way—for Bobby and possibly for you, too." Harris was quiet for several seconds. *"I want you to get your answers, but I don't want you to get them at such a high expense."*

"I know, and I promise I'm being safe. Now that I know I may be a potential target, I'm doing everything I can to steer clear of danger." Max smiled. "And thank you for caring, William. It means a lot."

"I do what I can. I'll be by later to get the stuff. Be safe."

"I will." He ended the call.

A loud banging from the entrance ripped a scream from Max. He whirled around, his heart racing. His hand moved involuntarily to the wound on his head. Adrenaline coursed through his veins, leaving him feeling giddy. *Yeah, I'm really prepared for danger. William would not be happy with me right now.*

The banging intensified, and Max realized it was from the front doors. *If this keeps up, I'm going to have a panic attack every time I come to or leave work. This is crazy!*

He looked left in the hallway to make sure the door to the free weights room was closed before stepping out and cautiously making his way to the entrance. As soon as the doors came in to view, the banging stopped.

"Hey, partner, your door's locked, and I need to work out," Jamie Robertson shouted.

And it didn't occur to you to read the sign three inches from your nose, telling you we're closed, did it? He waved at Jamie and hurried to the door. *It'll be less painful to just let him in and get it over with. I hope.*

Chapter Fifteen

Jamie burst through the door the second it became unlocked. "Why do you have the door locked? It's almost noon. And where is everyone? Did all the business with Skylar finally catch up to you, partner?"

Breathe. "We're actually closed," Max said, pointing at the sign Jamie had—most likely intentionally—not seen. "I'm doing some cleaning and checking to see if equipment needs to be repaired."

"Well, good for you. You have a head for numbers *and* for common sense. Don't see that much anymore, especially with your people these days. That Skylar kid was a mess, and don't even get me started on Corey. Am I right?" He slapped Max on the back with a laugh and turned it into putting his arm across Max's back to usher him down the hall. "Let's get you changed so I don't have to work out alone, what d'ya say?"

"I'm busy, Jamie," Max said. *Why do I let him get away with all this bigoted crap? I don't do it with anyone else.* "You feel free to use whatever you want. I'll work around you."

"Come on, Max. Do it for me," Jamie said. "That cleaning ain't going nowhere. It'll still be there when we're finished. Besides I need a man to talk to about man things. Being cooped up with that woman of mine day in and day out is torture at times. I swear you gays have got the right idea—no women." His laughter reverberated off the walls and down Max's spine.

Before Max realized it, they were in the locker room, and Jamie was dropping his bag on the bench. "Get yourself changed, partner, and we'll go work up a sweat," Jamie commanded.

Max opened his mouth to protest but turned away and walked to his locker. Jamie didn't want to hear anything other than "yes" anyway. *Just like always. God, how does Elaine put up with him? Why do I do it?*

As Max sat on the bench in front of his locker tying his shoes, Jamie walked up. "Hey, I want you to take a look at something. I've been hitting the weights pretty hard. What do you think?"

Max pulled his laces tight and looked up at Jamie, who was standing in front of him, naked from the waist up. "You've got some good definition going on. Looks like you're reaching your goal of cutting your body fat."

"Here, feel these." Jamie indicated his pectorals. "Oh, go on and feel. I know you're going to get a thrill out of it, but I'm—what is it you gays say?—secure in my sexuality. I can handle it."

Max suppressed a growl of frustration that Jamie would most likely spin into a growl of arousal. He stood up and quickly lay his palms flat against the other man's chest. *This is crazy.*

"Good work. I can definitely tell you've been working hard. Keep it up, and you'll have a nice body before too long. Um, which I'm sure Elaine will be happy about." He dropped his hands to his sides and quickly turned for the door.

Jamie fell in step behind him. "Shoot! I ain't doing this for her. This is for me! Tired of looking like a doughy, undercooked biscuit while the rest of you strut around like *GQ* models getting ready for a photo shoot. Hell, you and I are close to the same age, but you look even younger."

"Thanks," Max said. He led the way to the main workout room and started on the elliptical machines he knew Jamie favored as a warm-up. "So, what are your plans for today?"

"Whoa, big fella," Jamie said as he stepped onto his own machine and started it. "Just because I let you feel my boobs doesn't mean we're going steady or nothing." He laughed.

Max stripped off his own shirt and tossed it onto a machine in front of Jamie so the man would have no doubt what was happening. *Take a look at this, and we'll see whose 'boobs' are better. Jerk!* He intentionally flexed the muscles on his chest, stomach, and arms.

From the corner of his eye he saw Jamie look over and then stare straight ahead. *And that is how you shut someone up.* Max smiled smugly.

"So, what exactly did you tell Detective Harris to get him to go after Corey?" Max suppressed his own laugh when Jamie faltered and banged his knee against the side of the machine.

"Uh, what do you mean, partner? I wasn't talking to him about nothing like that," Jamie said.

"Look, I'm not mad or anything," Max soothed. "God knows I've had my fair share of issues with Corey. I just thought you might have had a reason for sic'ing the police on him."

"No reason," Jamie said. "I just told the detective what I knew, and apparently it was some things that Corey hadn't told him. It wasn't for no other reason than that."

"Don't worry about it. I'm not mad," Max reiterated. "I swear. We're still good, you and me." He reached over and patted Jamie on the back.

Max was thankful when Jamie remained quiet for the remainder of the warm up. Finally, he asked, "You ready to go hit some weights?"

"You bet." Jamie stabbed his finger into the "stop" button and practically leapt from the machine. He was out the door before Max's feet even touched the floor.

I probably shouldn't be enjoying making him uncomfortable. But I am! Max allowed himself a broad grin since Jamie wouldn't see it. When he got into the free weights room, Jamie was sitting on a bench with several decent sized weights on a bar.

"Come spot me, partner," Jamie said. "I want to see if I can bump up from my usual amount."

Max did a quick calculation of the weights and realized Jamie had stacked on an extra one hundred pounds from what he usually lifted. *I made an impression. Let's hope he doesn't kill himself to prove a point only he thinks is important.* He readied himself to prevent the potential suicide.

Max had to admit that Jamie surprised him. The man hit five reps before his face turned red enough to qualify as a stop sign. His sixth rep ended at his chest, but he was obviously refusing to ask for help. *Willing to die for ego. Why am I not surprised?*

Max reached down and started lifting the bar. He only exerted enough force to let Jamie think he was the one pushing the weights. When the bar was back in place, Jamie sat up and leaned forward.

"You okay?" Max asked.

"Fine, partner. That's a good burn, I tell you." Jamie took a few minutes before finally moving off to grab fifty pound barbells to work his biceps.

Max took up positon close by and continued the show. Jamie was pointedly not looking at him when he said, "So, Elaine said she might like to start using our membership after the first of the year. Do you mind helping get her going? She's kinda nervous."

"I'd be happy to," Max said. "I'll stop by The Vapor Trail later and talk to her. She's in pretty good shape already, regardless of what she thinks. We'll just help her get toned up."

"You're one of the good ones, Max," Jamie said. "I swear dealing with some of the other fa-ancy pants guys prancing around this place is almost unbearable sometimes. You aren't like that—not a typical gay."

Max knew it was supposed to be a compliment, no matter how underhanded it was. "You do realize not all gay men are alike, just like not all straight men? Right?"

"Oh, I know about your politically correct horse crap, and I don't want any of it. If that Skylar hadn't been such a—well, you know what I want to say—he'd probably still be alive right now." Jamie placed the weights back on the rack.

Max felt like moving back when the man came up and stood well within his personal space. *What is he doing?*

"I know I ain't exactly your favorite person, Max. I know I ain't exactly the most tactful or accepting person, neither." Jamie unnecessarily looked around. "But if you ever listen to anything I say, it should be this: That Corey is no good, and you would do well to get him out of here. That boy is mixed up in things that he shouldn't be, and it's going to start spilling over onto those around him."

Max stared at him. "Um, okay. Thanks, Jamie. Any particular reason you're telling me this? Do you need to tell me something specific?"

Jamie shook his head and stepped back to a comfortable distance. "I don't want to tell tales out of school. That's not my style. Just know that he's bad news."

Max waited for more, scrutinizing Jamie the entire time, but he didn't say anything else. "Well, thanks, again. I'll keep my eye on him. You want to work on your back today?"

"Naw, I think I've done enough for today. I'm going to hit the shower and get back to my store. Later, Max."

Max nodded and waved feebly.

That man is obviously on a seek-and-destroy mission. What the hell is going on around here? I was only gone two months!

Chapter Sixteen

Max finished the rest of his session. *Might as well do it while I can.* After retrieving his shirt from the machine where he had tossed it, he made his way to the locker room.

From the showers he could hear Jamie singing some country song. He didn't have too bad a voice, but his usual redneck twang made the words exaggerated almost to the point of being unknowable.

Max unlocked his locker and pulled out the mesh bag, stuffing his shirt inside. *I'll let Jamie finish and get out before I shower. I don't need more of his bigotry while I'm naked. That's too close to hell for my comfort.*

He looked around at all the lockers. Most of them had locks on the doors because they belonged to members of the gym. Walking to one that had no lock, he opened it. Someone had put a few pieces of trash inside, and he threw that away before feeling around the bottom panel.

Nothing. He moved to one a few steps down. The bottom of that one was intact as well. One after another he went through the empty lockers, and within five minutes he hadn't found a single one of them with a false bottom.

"Aaaaaalllll my exes live in Texas" echoed off the tiled shower walls, and Max turned around to stare in that direction. *I should record him and play it back. It sounds like he's killing a goat with an outboard engine.*

The water and singing turned off at the same time followed quickly by "Aw, shoot!" Wet feet slapped across the floor for a few seconds before Jamie poked his head around the corner to look into the locker room.

"Problem?" Max asked.

"Hey, partner, would you grab me a towel out of my locker? I forgot to get one before I got in here," Jamie said. "Needed some hot water on my muscles, you know?"

"Sure. What number is it?"

"Fifty-five. It's just there behind you," Jamie said, pointing.

"It's locked," Max said.

"The key's in my bag. Just keep your hands off my underwear." Jamie laughed.

That annoying, damnable laugh. He sounds like a jackass. He is a jackass. Max chuckled and rifled through the blue workout bag looking for the key.

"See, partner, there's that sense of humor. I knew I could bring it out eventually," Jamie crowed in victory.

"Yeah, funny," Max mumbled. He retrieved a towel from the locker after he'd opened it and carried it to Jamie. "I thought you might want these, too." He held out a pair of black-and-white striped boxer briefs.

"Couldn't resist, huh? You ornery little devil." Jamie snatched the underwear first, moved them into his hand hidden behind the wall, and then took the towel. "Thank you. I'll be out in a minute."

Max walked back to where he had been before helping out. He looked into the last locker he'd been inspecting. A thought hit him, and he turned around quickly.

Jamie's locker had a few things tossed in haphazardly, but for the most part it was fairly organized. Looking intently toward the door to the shower, Max ran his hand along the bottom panel. He could feel it moving slightly. His finger slid to the corner, and he lifted it up, looking underneath.

Plastic case. Bingo!

He quickly removed it, put the panel back into place, and shoved the case into the pocket of his shorts. He made it back to the empty locker mere seconds before Jamie came striding out with the towel slung over his shoulder.

"I figured the least I could do is give you a show since you were kind enough to help me," Jamie said smugly, smacking his own underwear-clad backside.

Max looked away and rolled his eyes. *I've seen and had better.* He ignored the sounds of Jamie dressing behind him and didn't turn around until he heard the locker door slam shut and the lock click into place.

"I'll walk you up front. Be sure to tell Elaine I'll be by in a little while," Max reminded him.

"Sure, partner. She'll be glad to see you." Jamie left the room ahead of Max and led the way. "Um, by the way, I, um, hope I didn't upset your fella too much at Crumbles the other day. I guess he just ain't used to my sense of humor yet."

"He isn't my 'fella,' but he's okay," Max said. "Just be careful what you say around him, and everything should be just fine."

They stopped in front of the doors, and Max leaned down to unlock it. When he stood back up, Jamie's outstretched hand was held near him. He looked at it briefly before staring quizzically at the man and grasping the hand in a firm shake.

"You're a decent guy, Max, gay or not. You've always treated me good, and I appreciate that." Jamie's voice sounded thick, and he cleared his throat. "I know people call me an ass behind my back. Thank you for putting up with me, and for helping me so much. Without you, my body and my business would be a flabby mess." He laughed and clapped Max on the back with his free hand.

"Um, wow, Jamie. Well, you're welcome," Max said. *Now who's the jackass?* "Take care."

"You, too," Jamie said. He stepped outside, waved, and walked the few feet to The Vapor Trail next door.

Max locked the door and walked back to the locker room. Once there, out of sight of anyone who could peer through windows or sneak up on him, he removed the case from his pocket and opened it.

Inside was a blank piece of paper.

Chapter Seventeen

"I think William is right," Max said around a mouthful of food. "You're going to fatten me up just in time for Christmas."

"Well, I have to compete with Henny," Kandy said. "I heard you've been cheating on me with her pumpkin cookies."

"I have no idea what you're talking about," Max deadpanned. "Besides, it all lies."

Kandy laughed. "Sure. So, speaking of delicious things, how *is* William doing?"

"You're terrible!" Max threw a piece of crust at her and shook his head when she snatched it out of the air and popped it into her mouth. "Well, he's doing well. I know I've probably said this before, but I still can't believe geeky, gawky Willie Harris grew up to be a hot, hunky cop."

"I seem to remember you mentioning it a few dozen times. Not that I'm counting or anything." She poured more coffee for both of them. "How does he feel about you playing amateur detective?"

"I'm not playing amateur anything," he said. "I *am* trying to figure out what is going on under my nose. I know it's drugs, but I'm not exactly one hundred percent sure what all that entails. Pot, most definitely. Is there a black market for insulin?"

"What?" Kandy asked. "I, um, don't think so. Although, given the crazy state of the world today, I could be wrong. Do you think Corey's been doing this all along, or just since Skylar came into the picture?"

Max shook his head. "I honestly don't know, although I suppose either is possible. My guess would be if he was doing it before, Skylar definitely opened the flood gates of opportunity."

"Poor Bobby," Kandy said.

"I hate that he was basically a fool in all this. Why couldn't he see what was going on?" Max asked.

"We don't see a lot of things when we're in the mix," Kandy said. She had that quirked eyebrow that meant she was trying to prove a point.

"I hate it when you give me the Vulcan look. What is it that you're trying to say without saying?" he asked.

"You didn't see it when Bobby was hurting and wrestling with whether to break up with you," she said. The words were soft and without recrimination, but they still slapped him in the face like a wet towel.

"I can't… Did you actually just—Kandy!" He stared at her, his hand held over his chest. *That actually hurts! My God!* "How could you say something like that?"

"Well, it wasn't to be mean," she promised, "but I think I've proven my point. You didn't see it coming with Bobby, and he didn't see it with Skylar. We tend to overlook things we don't want to see. I'm sure logically that Bobby knew Skylar was still using. He just chose to ignore it."

"Oh, you mean like I knew *logically* that Bobby was going to dump me, but I *chose* to ignore it? Kind of like that?" *I'm not going to cry. I'm not going to cry!*

Kandy took a deep breath and held it. "I didn't mean it that way, and you know it."

"Oh, I'm sure *logically* I know it, but I'm *choosing* to ignore it."

"You know that word I really don't like? Well, you're becoming that. Stop it." She reached across the table and snatched his quickly retreating hand as deftly as she had done with the piece of bread. "You didn't deserve what happened with Bobby, but, Max, sweetie, you had to have known it was coming. The writing was on the wall."

"What writing?" he shouted. "There was no writing! I thought we were doing fine. Stop it with the damned eyebrow! I come to you to talk and for comfort, and right now I wish I wasn't doing the one because I'm not receiving the other. I cannot believe you said that!"

"Max, I'm more than just a bit player in your life who happens to bring you delicious sandwiches and coffee when you feel like curling up in the fetal position and dying," she said.

"Stop using the soothing voice. I'm not a baby."

"It's for me, not for you," she said. She clenched his hand with both of hers. "You are my dearest friend—closer to me than anyone else. And you know that, Max. You just need to stop doing things for Bobby and start doing them for you."

"I'm looking into all this stuff for me, too. This is my livelihood. If the gym gets closed because of Corey being a drug-dealing idiot, I have no back-up plan," he said. "I have nothing. My whole life is tied up in that gym and…"

"And in Bobby," Kandy whispered.

Max wiped tears from his face with his free hand, but quickly had to move to napkins when the drops continued falling uncontrollably. "I hate this."

"You *need* this," she retorted. "Get it out. All of it. Get it out now so you can focus on you. And, hopefully, eventually, William. Because trust me, if you don't latch onto him, I'm going to do my best to turn him straight."

Max laughed in spite of his breaking heart. "Thank you. Thank you for always being there—for being my coffee-serving bit player." He wiped away the last of the tears. "God, life sucks sometimes."

"But not always," she reminded. "Better?"

"I'm getting there," he said with a slight nod. "Please promise me you won't serve up tears and heartache the next time I'm here. I've had my fill, thank you."

"I serve what my guests need." She winked, patted his hand, and then moved to the counter. "Speaking of which, I have a *pleasant* surprise for you."

Max's eyes widened when she sat a small plate in front of him. "Kandy, you're evil. Your homemade candied-pecan pie. You *are* trying to fatten me up!"

"Like a Christmas goose," she said. She kissed the top of his head and sat down again.

"If I die right now," he said with cheeks stuffed like a chipmunk's, "just bury me in this pie."

"That would be a waste."

He shoved another fork-full into his mouth and smiled when she smiled. "I'm sorry."

She waved it away while taking a drink of coffee. "You would tell me the same thing, and we both know it."

"With more tact," he said.

"Oh, please! You have the tact of a mongoose eating a cobra," she said while laughing.

"Ouch!" He pushed the last bite of pie into his mouth and licked the fork clean.

"I'll look away if you want to lick the plate, too," Kandy said.

"I hate you."

"Liar," she said.

"Oh my God! Barry! How long have you been standing there?" *And why aren't you wearing a bell so you can't sneak up on people?*

Barry stood a few feet away, staring down at the floor. When Max said his name, the man came close enough to stand behind an empty chair.

"You can sit down," Kandy said. Max wasn't sure if it was an invitation or a reminder for Barry on how his body worked around others.

"Thank you, but I don't want to intrude." He smiled and cast a quick glance at her from the corner of his eye. "I actually came to apologize to you, Max. I invited you to come see the dogs the other night, and then left when I… Well, I left suddenly."

Max pushed his plate away and turned on his phone so he could see the time. "I have to go talk to Elaine, but she'll be at work for a few more hours. Let's go, Barry. I've missed the babies."

Barry smiled wider than Max had seen in some time. "While you're there, I also have some pictures of foster dogs that you might want to think about adopting. Your life isn't complete without a dog. Or two."

Max pulled on his coat and kissed Kandy's cheek on his way out. "Thanks for the pie. I hope you saved me more."

"Possibly," she said with a wink.

Max walked to the front door and held it open for Barry. "Ok, let's talk *dog*. And I mean singular, as in one, Barry. I know what a smooth talker you are. If I'm not careful, you'll turn me into a crazy dog man in a matter of minutes."

Barry laughed and walked outside. "You can't blame a man for trying."

It's amazing, Max thought. *Get him talking about dogs, and it's like a whole different person. We just need to find him a human companion.*

"So, Barry, have you ever thought about—oh, I don't know—finding a friend with two legs who likes friends with four legs?" Max asked.

Chapter Eighteen

"You're just as cute as ever, aren't you?" Max held Sugar close to his chest and leaned his chin on her head as she nuzzled his neck.

"See, you really are a dog person." Barry held Num-Num close so she could lick Max's ear. "They love you. They can sense what a good person you are."

Max pulled away from Num-Num's tongue when she began darting it into his ear instead of just behind it. "Well, then it's no wonder they love you so much because you're the best person I know."

Barry turned red and shook his head. "I don't know about that, but I appreciate the thought." He placed his dog gently on the floor and watched her bound across the floor toward the back.

Max followed suit and gratefully accepted the wet-wipe Barry offered him, wiping his face and ear vigorously. "They are just the cutest. So, how's business, Barry? Your books are looking good."

"Thank you. I truly can't complain. Everything is steady, and we have a waiting list a mile long." He led Max into the office where he pulled a small brown book from a shelf. "These are the foster dogs I was telling you about. A friend of mine runs a local rescue—one of many, unfortunately—and they are constantly looking for homes for the dogs they take in."

Max accepted the book and started thumbing through the pages. *I can't believe people do this to animals they supposedly love.* "Wow, there really are a lot of them."

"There are even more than that," Barry said. "It breaks my heart to see all those sad faces. I meant what I said earlier, you really would do well with a dog of your own. Something small you could take with you to the gym—a mascot, maybe?"

"We already have a mascot, and I don't think Corey would like the competition." Max chuckled but stopped when he saw Barry just staring at him. "Sorry."

"I think you're too hard on him," Barry said. He immediately turned red and looked down at his feet, wringing his hands slowly.

"Don't do that, Barry."

"Do what?" He still refused to make eye contact.

"It's okay for you to be assertive and tell people what you think and feel without being embarrassed or afraid." Max laid the book on the desk, leaving it open to the last page he'd looked at. "You shouldn't be ashamed of what you have to say."

"Most people don't want to hear it," Barry said. He shrugged and backed up to the bookshelf.

"Most people don't want to hear what most other people have to say," Max said. "That doesn't keep people from saying it, though. Barry, you're an intelligent man with great business sense and a heart made of the purest gold. You need to let yourself shine instead of always caving in on yourself."

Barry slowly lifted his head until he made eye contact. "I do mean it, though. Corey is a nice person. Sure he has his flaws—like all of us—but that doesn't change the fact that deep down he's good. He just has damage that you've never seen."

Max stared at Barry like he was truly seeing him for the first time. "You've hidden who you are so well, Barry, that I'm afraid to admit I don't really know you."

Barry smiled and turned red, but he maintained eye contact. "That could be said for everyone."

"So, what do you know about Corey that I'm not seeing?" Max asked.

"Oh, that's not for me to tell," Barry said. "You really should try to talk to Corey about it. It's amazing what you can find out and what people are willing to say when a willing listener is present."

"And you do a lot of listening." Max sat in the extra chair and smiled when Barry casually sat in his own chair. "I guess I'm not such a good person after all, huh?"

"Oh, that's not what I meant." Barry looked at Max, horror clearly written on his face until he saw the easy smile Max was directing at him. "I think you're the best of us. You certainly seem better put together."

Max laughed. "If you only knew. If you only knew. I'm sure you heard me talking to Kandy."

"At least Kandy gives you the benefit of the doubt and lends you her shoulder," Barry said. "Corey needs that, too, and I think you're the one he wants it from. You're like a big brother to him. He just doesn't understand why you don't like him."

"I don't—" Max cut himself off before the lie could leave his tongue. "Wow. Okay." He scrubbed his face with his hands. "I have got to talk to him. *Really* talk to him, I mean. He's just always annoyed me, and I've never bothered to sit down with him and see him as a human being."

"It's easy to take people for granted." Barry held the dog book out to Max. "But that's one thing dogs never do."

Max laughed and accepted the book. "You're smart *and* devious Barry Flinn. So, why haven't you got someone in your life?"

Barry turned redder than Max had ever seen him turn before. He started stammering; his words tripping over one another so frantically that it was anyone's guess what they actually were.

Max reached out and patted Barry's shoulder reassuringly. "Hey, it's okay. I'm sorry. I didn't mean to get you that worked up."

Barry took a deep breath. Sugar ran up to him, and he pulled her into his lap, petting her and obviously soothing himself in the process.

When he started breathing normally, Barry said, "It makes me too nervous. I start wondering who would want someone like me, and then it devolves into a vicious circle of self-doubt and judgment that ends with me just holding a dog on my lap. Nobody wants that. Nobody wants a balding, forty-something in their life."

"Barry, you're a good looking guy, and I think we've covered the heart of gold. You need to give yourself more credit." *He is just the cutest thing when he blushes. That'll get him far,* Max thought. "So, is there anyone you have your eye on? A lucky lady? Or guy?"

"Maybe," Barry whispered. "I just…don't want to talk about it. Not yet. Okay?"

"Not a problem. You just know that I'm here for you whenever you need me," Max reassured him.

"Thanks. One thing I could do with is some workout advice. *If* you have time." Barry set Sugar onto the floor, and she scampered away, barking.

Max looked at the time on his phone. "I'll tell you what, why don't you come in tomorrow morning. I promised I'd meet with Elaine today, but you and I can work something out tomorrow. No pun intended."

"Sure. Thanks." Barry refused to take back the dog book when Max attempted to hand it to him. "No, keep it. Look through it and find someone. If you don't see one there you like, let me know. I can find others."

Max tucked the book under his arm. "Thanks. I'll see you in the morning."

They shook hands, and Max left Biscuit Acres. *What am I getting myself into? Accountant, business owner, match maker, and probably dog owner—why do I do this to myself?!*

Chapter Nineteen

Max walked along the sidewalk toward The Vapor Trail. The air had started becoming chilly as the sun dipped closer and closer to the horizon. *Winter in Oklahoma—seventies during the day and twenties at night. I really need to get out of this place.*

He stopped briefly in front of My Parents' Basement to look at the holiday display Zane had put together. The heroes from different comic universes were battling it out over a ceramic nativity scene with baby Superman in his spaceship in place of the manger.

Zane caught his eye through the window and smiled, offering a huge thumbs-up which Max returned before waving. *Oh, if Elizabeth Walker sees that little scene she will flip out. There'll be so many Bibles in front of that store Zane will think the Baptist convention set up on his doorstep.*

Carheart Insurance was already closed for the day. Max hadn't seen Daniel Carheart since before leaving for Barbados. He had brought up his concerns to Eden, who had told him Daniel had been sick and was slowly recovering.

I just had to invoke her memory! Max thought when Eden opened her door and stuck her head out.

"Max, could you be a dear and come help me with something, please and thank you?" She beckoned him in, and the door slowly closed when she walked away without waiting for his response.

"I'm never going to get to talk to Elaine," he grumbled. He stepped inside, inhaling deeply the scents of pine, cinnamon, and cranberries. *This really is a Garden of Eden.*

"Back here," Eden called out to him from her store room behind the main counter.

He maneuvered around beautiful flower arrangements that, at first glance, appeared to have exploded randomly around the store. However, when he looked back from the doorway to the store room, he could see the method to Eden's madness. She had the store set up in such a way that colors subtly blended from one to another, drawing the potential customer toward the point-of-sale.

"How do you do it?" he asked. "I couldn't do this if my life depended on it."

"Some of us are just gayer than others, Max." She hugged him before dragging him into the room. "The delivery men made a mess of things today, and Jamie said he would help me out, but I think he has his hands full." She indicated boxes stacked on top of boxes in the center of the floor. "Could you be a dear and put those two large ones on that shelf? I can manage the rest, but those are just too heavy."

"I saw him earlier at the gym," Max said. He put the dog book on a chair just inside the door and squatted down to grab the first box. He lifted it easily from the floor and put it in its place. "He didn't seem too busy then."

"Stop and listen," Eden said. She had moved up to him and put her hand on his arm, stopping him in his tracks. The index finger of her left hand was held to her own lips.

At first Max didn't hear anything but soon the sound of raised voices slowly penetrated the wall. He turned his head to better hear, but still only snippets of sentences were discernable. There was no denying, however, that Jamie and Elaine Robertson had engaged in a heated argument.

"It's happening more and more. They've never argued as much as they have over the past few months." She squeezed his arm and shook her head, sadness clearly written on her face. "I'm afraid our little family is about to become broken."

"You think they're getting divorced?" Max asked. He couldn't believe it, but the vehemence and anger in the words thrown back and forth was undeniable. "Wow. This is so sad. I guess I shouldn't have been surprised given the little sniping show they were putting on Saturday night."

A loud sound that was most likely a slap was followed by curse words that were undeniably distinct. Max wondered who had slapped who.

"I can't just stand here and let this happen. Be prepared to call the police." He quickly placed the other box on the shelf and ran out of the store. Eden shouted something behind him, but he couldn't hear what she said.

As he walked briskly between Garden of Eden and The Vapor Trail, the latter's door burst open, and Jamie—sporting a huge red mark on his left cheek—stormed to his truck. Max stopped and watched as the furious man squealed his tires on his way out of the parking lot and blew through the red light at Skelly Drive.

He started to go back to tell Eden everything was over, but he saw she had stuck her head out the door, witnessed the aftermath of the fight, and stepped back inside.

Now, do I go talk to Elaine or pretend I forgot and do it tomorrow? He struggled with the choices for a while before finally settling on going into the store.

Christmas music played quietly, and the door chime had been changed from the annoying *bing-bong* to an even more annoying sound of sleigh bells that he thought would never stop. The store was empty—*No surprise there, with the knock-down-drag-out fight going on*—and Max slowly walked toward the counter.

"I thought I told—" Elaine's words died when she saw Max. She turned around, but not before he had seen her red eyes and dripping mascara. "Oh, Max. Jamie said you'd be by. Give me just a minute to freshen up. I've had some rather bad news, and I look like a raccoon." She disappeared back into the office she had stormed out of.

Max shook his head sadly. He walked through the store, looking at the products and giving Elaine time to put a better face on herself and her situation.

He had never really bothered to look through the store before, and was struck by the different types of devices and the liquids available. *Who smokes grape-flavored anything? That's disgusting!*

"Okay, all better now," Elaine said. She stepped up to the counter with a smile Max could tell she didn't feel. "How's it going?"

"I'm well. How are you?" He tried to make the question not sound loaded, but felt like he hadn't succeeded.

"I'm great." If she thought anything about what he said, she apparently chose to ignore it. "So, you think you can whip this body into shape?"

"Not much whipping needed," Max said. *Focus on this, not on the fight. It's none of your business.* "You look great, and we both know it—even if I am the only one willing to admit it."

"You flatterer," she responded. Her new smile was genuine. "Go make yourself comfortable in the office. I'm going to lock up, and then I'll be in. Kandy just brought a carafe of Christmas spice coffee if you'd like a cup."

"I would love one. It's getting bitter cold out there again." He removed his gloves and jacket on his way into the office and tossed them onto a chair. The delicious aromas of coffee and spices filled the air when he poured a cup full.

"Oh, that smells amazing," Elaine said as she came in behind him. "Would you mind pouring a cup for me? Thank you." She accepted the cup he held out to her.

"Thank you for sharing." He settled into a chair, thankful his jacket provided a buffer between him and the cold plastic. "When do you want to start at the gym? You and Jamie have been paying for joint membership for some time now."

A dark cloud moved across her face when he mentioned Jamie's name. It was something else they both chose to ignore.

"Well, with Christmas coming quickly now wouldn't be a good time, but after the New Year," she said. "I just don't want this to be one of those resolutions that everyone makes and then forgets about before February."

"If we start slowly and build up to it with small goals, I think you'll be better off. Rushing into it is what trips most people up," he said.

"Like so many things in life," she muttered.

"Um, yeah." He shifted uncomfortably in his seat and sipped from the coffee. "So, how do you feel about the first Monday of the month? We can do three days a week for about thirty minutes. That's a good starting place."

"Sounds great." She looked off to the side and stared at the wall, seemingly forgetting he was there.

"Elaine, are you okay? I'm not trying to intrude, but you seem really upset." *You're supposed to not be getting involved!* "I'm sorry. Forget I said anything."

She waved away his concern. "I'm just realizing how little I truly know someone, and it hurts like hell. It's almost like being betrayed." She wrapped both hands around her coffee cup and took a drink. "Maybe I need to go to Barbados for a couple months."

"That's a two-edged sword, let me tell you." He leaned forward and rested his elbows on the desk; his coffee steamed beneath his mouth. "I'm here for you if you ever want to talk, okay?"

Elaine wiped away a tear and smiled sadly. "You're very sweet to offer. There's just so much and so little I can or want to say. We all make decisions and do things we think are right at the time, but when clarity sets in, we realize how misguided we were. I'm just hitting that point with several things."

"Decisions or mistakes can be corrected," he offered.

"Not all of them," she whispered. "We do what we can to protect ourselves, and our loved ones. But what do we do when we need to protect them from themselves, or—even worse—from us?"

How do I even answer that? This has landed in territory I never expected. "Elaine, did Jamie hurt you?"

"We've hurt each other so much that I can't keep track anymore," she said. "The emotional hurts worse than the physical, and sometimes the lack of one leads to even worse hurt."

What does that even mean? "Are you going to be okay? I can drive you home if you want. Maybe we could go have a light dinner with Kandy?"

Elaine seemed to be thinking about it for a few minutes before shaking her head. "No, but thank you, Max. You're very sweet to offer. Jamie will be back soon, and we'll finish the dance the way we always do, and life will go on. Que sera, sera."

"I could bring you something," he offered.

"Do you and that handsome detective have any plans?" she asked.

Well, I guess that answers that. "We don't have any plans because we're not together. Besides, he's working on several cases. You know what the murder rate is like in Tulsa."

"All too well," she said. "Well, you go enjoy your evening and let me get back to enjoying my life."

Ouch! "Well, if you *do* need anything, you have my number, and you're more than welcome to call. It's no bother." He put his now-empty cup on the desk and pulled on his coat and gloves.

Crap, I forgot the dog book. Maybe Eden will still be there. He offered to wash the cup before leaving, but Elaine told him not to worry about it. She followed him to lock the door behind him.

"Oops, looks like someone dropped this." He bent down and picked up an e-cig from the floor. "Looks like Corey's." He held up the slim device for Elaine to see.

She took it from him, saying, "It's a popular model. Jamie probably dropped it on his way out. Thanks." She tucked it into a pocket.

Max opened the door and stepped outside, instantly shivering. "Shoot me if I ever get used to this cold."

"You and me both," Elaine said. "Good night, Max."

"Good night."

Chapter Twenty

Saturday morning—I remember when those were for lying in bed, snuggling, and not worrying about the world until at least one o'clock. Reality sucks!

Max leaned his chin on the steering wheel of his Jeep and stared at the doors to Tight/Fit. *I think I've been in this position before.* It was hard to believe it had been only a little over a week since he returned from Barbados to a world gone topsy-turvy.

He heard Jamie Robertson's truck pulling into the parking lot. The Dodge came to a stop, and then revved his engine a couple of times like a teenaged boy showing off for his pals. His passenger side window rolled down, and he shouted something, but Max couldn't hear it over the noise.

"I asked if you wanted to get a cup of coffee before we started our day," Jamie said once he had turned off his truck and Max had stepped out of his Jeep.

I'd rather be eaten by wolves and be conscious the whole time. "Sounds great," he said. "Kandy usually has a cup waiting for me about now."

They walked toward the opposite end of the strip mall in silence. Jamie thrust his hands into the pockets of his coat and retracted his head like a turtle. *Please, just let him keep this light and friendly. I don't know if I can handle an in-depth conversation after what I heard the other night.*

Max held the door for Jamie, who stood back and indicated Max should go in first. They remained locked in a politeness tug of war for a few seconds before Max finally relented and went ahead.

"Close the damned door," John Gallowylde bellowed from a table off to the side. "I'm in here to get warm and away from that woman, not to have myself frozen to the bone."

"Good morning, John," Max and Jamie said in unison.

John grunted in response, shook his newspaper like he was trying to dislodge money from the pages, and held it up like a screen, effectively shutting out the world.

The two men exchanged knowing glances and smiles before finding a table of their own. Kandy took their drink orders and went to fill them, and Max checked the time on his phone.

Fifteen minutes. How much can he talk about in fifteen minutes?

"So, Elaine said you stopped by the other night." Jamie unzipped his jacket and pulled it open, obviously getting comfortable. "She said you two are going to start working together after the New Year. Thanks for doing that. She's really looking forward to it."

"You're welcome. Anything to help a friend." Max thanked Kandy for the coffee.

"So, um, as a friend, I was wondering if I could discuss some things with you," Jamie said. He looked around, apparently wanting to make sure Kandy was out of earshot again and that Mr. Gallowylde was still immersed in his paper.

Me and my big mouth. Great job, Maximillian. "Sure. What's going on?" He blew across the top of his coffee and gingerly sipped at the hot liquid while enjoying the strong aroma tickling his nose.

"Well, you see, Elaine and I…well, we aren't exactly seeing eye to eye right now." Jamie fidgeted in his chair, apparently attempting to find a comfortable spot that didn't exist for him. His eyes firmly latched onto his coffee cup.

"That happens," Max said. "These things pop up and blow over more all the time. Surely this isn't the first time you guys have had a disagreement?"

"Oh, we've had plenty of them. You don't have peace and quiet from two people who have strong personalities." Jamie laughed, but Max could tell it wasn't his usual jovial guffaw that made people want to hit him. "This is just the first time that I've been afraid it might be the end, you know?"

"I hope it isn't, Jamie—truly—but sometimes there is no stopping some things once they've started." Max looked at his phone. *Why is eight o'clock taking so long to get here?*

"I don't think I can handle it if Elaine leaves me, Max. I hate to admit that you're stronger than I am, but if I was you and having to deal with the fact that Bobby dumped me, I wouldn't make it." Jamie shook his head, his eyes wide but still focused on the coffee the entire time. "You're tough, partner. Tougher than I'll ever be, but don't tell anyone I said so."

Yeah, wouldn't want the gay man to be tougher than you, huh? Max resisted the temptation to roll his eyes and forced himself to channel sympathy instead of ire. *Even when he's hurting and wanting help he's being a jackass. God!*

Max took a deep breath and bit off the words on the end of his tongue, forming new ones in their place. "We're all strong in our own ways. Have either of you done something that you can't come back from?"

"Elaine? God, no. That woman's a saint. She doesn't get even, she just gets hurt. She's a sensitive soul. She takes and takes and takes until she snaps, but God help you when she does." Jamie rubbed at his cheek, not knowing that Max had seen the hand print Elaine had left behind.

"And, um, what about you?" Max saw the look on Jamie's face. "I'm sorry. I'm prying, and I don't mean to. You don't have to answer."

"No, no. It's okay." Jamie made eye contact for the first time since they sat down. "I'm ashamed of what I've done, Max, and I don't know if I can forgive myself for it. How can I expect Elaine to forgive me?"

"You said yourself she's pretty long-suffering. I'm sure she can find it in her heart to forgive you," Max offered.

Jamie shook his head. "I don't think so. Not for this."

"Is it really that bad?" *For the love of God, just tell me!*

"It's bad," Jamie whispered.

Max felt his stomach clench into a knot. "Jamie, did you kill Skylar?"

"What?!" Jamie rocketed to his feet. In the process, his knees banged the table, toppled the coffee cups, and spilled liquid across the entire surface. "Is that what you think this is about? You think I murdered that little fag and had so much guilt built up inside me that I had to come unburden myself to you? How dare you?"

"Is there a problem?" Kandy threw two towels on the table and looked pointedly at Max. He was busy attempting to get away from the hot java waterfall cascading onto his pants and didn't realize she had directed the question at him.

"You're damn right there's a problem here!" Jamie shouted. "The pansy here thinks I murdered that worthless piece of crap, Skylar, and that I'm trying to confess to it." Jamie hastily zipped his coat and pushed the chair back so forcefully that it tipped over. The sound of wood crashing into stone tile filled the coffee shop.

"That is *more* than enough," Kandy said. She hadn't raised her voice, and that fact caught Max's attention immediately.

"It's okay. He's upset. Let him blow off some steam," Max said.

"Screw you," Jamie said. "I don't need you sticking up for me after having the nerve to accuse me of murder. I'll tell you this," he said, poking his finger at Max across the still-flooded table, "whoever did kill that little nancy piece of crap did the world a favor."

Max shot to his feet, but Kandy pushed him back down without looking at him. She stared intently at Jamie. "It's time for you to leave. And don't you dare think about coming back until you've apologized to Max, to Mr. Gallowylde, and to me, Jamie Robertson. You're not welcome here until you do."

"I don't want to be in this damn place anyhow." Jamie brushed past her on his way to the door. He stopped midway across the threshold and turned back, again stabbing his finger in the air like a missile looking for a target. "And don't think about sending your new boyfriend after me neither. I don't care if he is a cop. He comes near me, I'll stomp a mud hole in his ass, good and deep." He stormed off into the bitter cold morning.

"Well, that's what I get for opening my big mouth," Max said. He grabbed one of the towels and began sopping up the mess from the table. "Sorry about this."

"Not your mess to apologize for," Kandy said. She took up the other towel and started working on the floor. "Do you honestly think he killed Skylar?"

"I don't know if he did or not, but I honestly thought that was what he was going to confess to." Max stared at the wet spots on his jeans. *Glad I have clothes to change into at the gym. Crap!* He pulled his phone out and checked the time. "I have to go open; I'm already late."

"Go. I've got this. Do you want me to bring you another cup later?" she offered.

"I'll come get it." He kissed her on the cheek and left the shop, jogging down the sidewalk toward Tight/Fit.

"Well, it's about time," Elizabeth Walker said. She was dancing around to keep her blood circulating. "I've been standing out here for two minutes."

"Good morning," Max said. He fumbled the keys from his pocket and unlocked the door.

"It was until I got here." She pushed past him and stormed down the hall toward the aerobics room.

"Why couldn't someone have murdered her?" Max mumbled. He immediately felt guilty. *Every time I accuse Jamie of being a jackass, I prove I'm as much of one as well. God, am I really that bad?*

He repeatedly massaged his temples on his way to the locker room to change out of his wet pants. Walking past aerobics, he heard Elizabeth Walker talking on her cell phone, telling some unfortunate soul he was fired.

Chapter Twenty-One

"Okay, that's it for today. I'll see you all on Monday. Good job, everyone." Max wiped sweat from his forehead with a towel and draped it over his neck. He took a long drink of water, enjoying the soothing sensation it brought to his throat. It had been a while since he had led an aerobics class.

Yet another reason to miss Bobby. He spoke briefly to those people who said "goodbye" on their way out of the class before deciding to go do a further cool down on the treadmill.

The Saturday morning crowd was definitely out in full force, but he found a machine without a problem. He had been walking for a few minutes when someone stepped onto the machine next to him.

"Hey, Barry, decided to get an early start on things, huh?" He checked the man out briefly. "Looking good. You've still got great definition, even though you haven't been to the gym in a while."

Barry blushed and fumbled through programming the machine. He almost stumbled when the belt started moving beneath his feet, and the redness in his cheeks deepened further.

"Careful. No gym road kill allowed." Max smiled to take any potential sting from his words, but he could tell he had embarrassed Barry more. "It's okay. Lighten up. Don't take everything so seriously."

"I wasn't always like this," Barry said. He glanced at Max quickly before staring resolutely at the display in front of himself.

"I'm not going to pry, but I will tell you that you have a heart of gold, and you have a lot to offer to any relationship. Some woman is going to be very happy she met you, just wait and see."

"It could potentially be a man, too," Barry said.

"Alright, Barry." Max clapped him on the back. "I had no idea."

"Just don't tell anyone. Please." Barry looked directly at Max, pleading strongly evident in his eyes. "You know how people get about the whole bi thing. I'm just not ready to deal with that."

"Sure. No problem," Max assured him. "However, if I'm going to help you with making yourself the total package, we're going to have to have some rules.

"Rule number one is no talking or thinking badly about yourself anymore. You *are* a great catch, whether you think so or not, and we've already covered the heart of gold. You need to start believing that, and working on strengthening your self-esteem as much as you do for your body.

"Rule number two is you're in charge. We go at the pace you want to, and I will only push if I think you need it. This has to be something you want for yourself, not something I want for you.

"Rule number three is always feel free to come to me for anything. If you need me, I'm here. You have my number. You know my schedule. There's no reason why you shouldn't be able to talk to me if you need it. Are you okay with all that?"

Barry nodded and stood a little straighter on the treadmill. "Thank you, Max. This means a lot to me."

"You're welcome." He stopped his treadmill, and then reached over to do the same to Barry's. "We'll start right now. No more Mr. Mouse. From now on it's Barry the Tiger."

Barry laughed. "I'm going to do my best, I promise."

"That's all I ask," Max said. "So, I want you to go over to the circuit area. I'm going to get some evaluation forms from my office so we can set your regimen. I'll be back in a few minutes."

As Max left the main workout area, he heard a woman shouting. It became louder the closer he got to his office, until he finally saw Elizabeth Walker standing in front of the reception counter. Her arms bounced around like a car salesman's inflatable while she verbally attacked the attendant on duty.

"Melissa, is there a problem?" He stepped behind the counter and saw the instant relief that flooded over the young woman's face.

"Yes, there's a problem," Elizabeth said. "I have been trying to get it through her thick skull that I am very dissatisfied with how I have been treated by this place over the past week."

"Melissa, why don't you take a break while I speak with Mrs. Walker?" He smiled reassuringly at her. "Oh, would you please stop by the circuit area and tell Barry Flinn that I'll be with him as soon as possible? Thanks."

He waited for Melissa to get safely away before addressing Elizabeth. "What seems to be the problem?"

"There is no seeming to it," she seethed. "Over the past week I have had the worst experiences and service from this place. First, I find a dead body. I am still having nightmares about that, I must tell you. Then, if that wasn't bad enough, you close in the middle of the week with almost zero notice, and then I have to freeze to death this morning waiting for you."

She leaned on the countertop. "And I was trying to get that stupid girl of yours to understand that all of this is terribly unacceptable, but she was anything but willing to be helpful. I am telling you, if this continues I *will* be taking my business elsewhere, and I promise there are a lot of people here who will come with me when I leave. This place will be a ghost town."

Actually, when people find out you're no longer here, I'll probably have customers hanging from the rafters. He kneeled down and retrieved a red folder from a drawer and placed it in front of her.

"I truly am sorry for what you've gone through," he said. "As I'm sure you can attest this has been a week far from the norm for us. However, I'm going to give you a gift certificate good for one week of tanning and massage. All you have to do is present it to the attendant here or in the tanning area, and they'll take care of you from there."

He completed the certificate and held it out for her. However, when she grabbed it, he didn't let go. "Elizabeth, I know this has been a bad week—for all of us. I also understand that this isn't exactly how you wanted this situation resolved. It is what it is. I assure you that Monday morning you will not be waiting for someone to unlock the doors past opening time."

He leaned forward and stared intently at her. "We are moving forward from this unfortunate incident. *However*, I assure you that if you ever treat me or my staff with anything but the utmost respect ever again, I will put you out of here so fast that your buns of steel will crack the concrete."

He released the small piece of paper and stepped into his office without waiting for her response. When he retrieved the evaluation forms and walked past reception, Elizabeth Walker was nowhere to be seen.

Probably not the best way to handle that, but I'm sick and tired of that woman!

He found Barry in the circuit area, waiting patiently, and apologized for taking so long. They worked their way through all the machines. Barry did as much weight as he could on each one, and Max made notes. When they finished, they reviewed the workout routine.

"This is going to be the best way to start," Max assured. "Let's go to my office, and I'll make you a copy of this so you can have it."

"You have no idea how much I appreciate you doing this," Barry said.

"It's what friends are for." *I should probably avoid saying stuff like that after what happened with Jamie.*

In the office, Max copied the paper and handed it to Barry, who read over it. He thanked Max and gave him a quick kiss on the cheek.

"Is this a private party, or can anyone join in?"

Max looked at William Harris standing in the doorway and smiled. "Hey, you."

Barry began stammering and collapsed into himself like a heavy star.

"It's okay." Harris smiled at Barry and gently squeezed his shoulder. "We're not together. Besides, I'm not the jealous type."

"I didn't mean anything by it. I swear," Barry said. His color slowly receded back to normal from fire-engine red.

"Do you need anything else, Barry?" Max asked. When the man shook his head, Max said, "I'll see you sometime Monday, then."

Barry thanked him, said his goodbyes, and hastily left the office.

Harris chuckled as he pulled a folded bundle of papers from his inside jacket pocket. "Merry Christmas. I'm not sure you're going to like your present, though." He tossed the bundle onto Max's desk.

Max sat in his chair, contemplatively eyeing the present. "Is it Skylar's toxicology report or the lab results from Corey's stuff?"

Harris cast a skeptical look at him. "I think we covered the M.E.'s office quagmire already."

"That's what I was afraid of." Max picked up the papers. "Do I even want to know?"

"Probably not," Harris said. He sat on the corner of the desk. "Still, you're going to have to do something because I really don't have a legal leg to stand on."

Max nodded and opened the bundle. He spent a few minutes reading before throwing them back on the table. "I'm going to kill him."

Chapter Twenty-Two

Max attempted to brush past Harris, who grabbed his arm and forced him to a stop. He looked down at the strong hand gripping him then into Harris's deep eyes, which melted away some of his anger.

"Do you think this is a good idea?" Harris asked.

"I'm not really going to kill him," Max said. "Although, that's exactly what I want to do. He has to answer for this."

"There are better ways to go about it," Harris said. "There are ways that will allow *me* to do something about it. As it is right now, it's your word against his based on something we can't actually pin on him. You don't have any weight to your accusation."

"That's not what's important to me right now. He's brought this crap into my gym," Max said. He pulled out of Harris's grip. "I don't want him going to jail, but this *will* stop today—one way or another." He continued out of the office.

He blew into the juice bar like a hurricane hitting land and scanned the room. It was empty. *I swear he has radar when it comes to trouble. I just wish he ran away from it more often.* He turned around and bumped into Harris.

"Sorry. I can handle this, you know. I don't need you to provide supervision," Max said. He hated that his tone sounded so harsh, but the anger seeped through.

"I have no doubt. I'm just here for moral support," Harris said.

Max briefly smiled his appreciation before the storm picked up speed again and carried him down the hall. He went from room to room. People apparently saw the intensity in his eyes because they either avoided him or got out of his way as quickly as they could. Finally, he stepped into the locker room, immediately locking eyes with his prey.

"Hey, Max." Corey smiled, but it widened when he saw Harris. "*Hello*, Detective. Always a pleasure to see you, honey."

"Not today," Harris mumbled, but only Max heard it.

Before Corey realized what was happening, Max had him pressed against a locker—one hand firmly against his shoulder, the other holding the papers in his hand like a talisman against evil.

"What is this, Corey? Why did you bring this into my gym?" Max shouted.

"Ow, honey, calm down. You're hurting m—Ow!" Corey attempted to move forward, but Max pressed him back.

"Answer me!"

"Max, calm down," Harris said softly.

"What's wrong with you?" Corey demanded. "Get him off me. This is assault and battery."

"Assault, yes," Max growled, "but we haven't gotten to the battery part yet. Now, look at this and tell me why you deserve to keep your job after *this!*"

Corey stopped his struggle and ripped the pages from Max's hand. He read for a few seconds before glaring back at his employer. "You lied to me."

"You lied first," Max shot back.

Corey opened his mouth, but his eyes immediately darted to Harris. "I'm not saying anything in front of a cop."

"He's not here to be a cop. He's here to keep me from doing something you'll regret," Max said. He tightened his grip on Corey's shoulder.

Corey shook his head. "He's a cop, first and foremost, no matter what you say. I'm not stupid, honey, even though you do think so. If you want answers, he leaves."

"You have no right to make demands right now," Max said.

"Maybe not, honey, but I'm in the best position. You want answers. I want him out of it." Corey crossed his arms. "Besides, you stole something that rightly belongs to me, and the fact that it's a prescription medication means that if I press charges, your boyfriend isn't getting you out of it—cop or not."

"I'm not his boyfriend, but he's right, Max," Harris said.

Max stared daggers at Harris, but he knew he was stuck. Slowly he released Corey and backed away. "My office. Now. And if you even think about leaving before we've settled this, I will hunt you down and not even the hosts of hell will be able to restrain me."

"Wow, honey, chill out." Corey stepped past Max and told Harris, "This one—what a ferocious tiger. Me-ouch!" He disappeared through the door.

"If you *don't* end up killing him, I'll be amazed. Not because I think you lack control," Harris said, "but because his mouth pretty much begs it to happen."

"Tell me about it." Max put his hands on Harris's shoulders. "Thank you for supporting me, even though I know you don't agree with how I'm doing this. It means a lot to me, William."

"You're welcome," Harris said. "Call me if you need anything—except bail money. You're on your own for that."

"Duly noted," Max said. "Now, get out of here. I don't need any witnesses."

Chapter Twenty-Three

"I can't believe you thought I was actually going to say anything to you in front of Detective Harris," Corey said. He sat in Bobby's chair, swiveling back and forth. The papers lay on the desk in front of him.

Max sank into his own chair. *One. Two. Three.* He pulled up to the desk and stared across at Corey. *Four. Five. Six.* The counting started over when Corey just stared at him.

"I didn't expect you to be doing illegal crap in my gym. Steroids, Corey. You seriously thought it was okay to push steroids?" Max shook his head. "Why would you do that?"

"I do run a juice bar, honey," Corey said. The grin on his face became knowingly infuriating.

"Enough!" Max shouted. "You've been going back and forth like a yo-yo over the past few days. So much so that I don't even know you anymore. What the hell is wrong with you?"

Corey took a deep breath. The grin didn't return. After a few minutes of silence, he finally said, "Max, let's face the facts of the matter. You never really knew me at all."

"What?"

Corey shook his head. "You know I'm right, honey. You've never really known me. I don't fit into the perfect picture you had painted of what life should be like here. You're clueless, and you don't like the fact that I don't fit into the mold of what you want me to be. My personality and individuality are an affront to you."

"What does that have to do with you selling steroids in my gym?" Max demanded. "I don't care who you are, but your actions are unacceptable. They may have even resulted in Skylar being killed by whoever you two were mixed up with in your little drug ring."

"First of all, it was hardly a 'drug ring.' Secondly, Skylar had no idea about the steroids. It was something I was doing entirely on my own," Corey said. "Skylar was more into pot, coke, and meth. Pot I get. The others are crazy. I had no desire to break bad with him."

"But you didn't have a problem with the money," Max said.

"Oh, God, no." Corey laughed and shook his head. "Honey, do you have any *idea* how much money that little queen was hauling in? It was a king's ransom. Why wouldn't I want a taste of that?"

"Regardless, you're admitting that the steroids were yours?" Max asked.

"To you, yes," Corey said. "But I'm not about to tell that delicious detective of yours. At this point, it's your word against mine, and that's how I like it."

Max stared at him, finally realizing Corey was right. He had never really known the man. "How many people here are your customers?"

"Not many," Corey said. "None that you would suspect."

"Jamie Robertson?" Max asked. "I found the container in his locker."

"What container?" Corey asked.

"The plastic container under the bottom plate of his locker," Max said. "The one with the blank piece of paper in it."

"That's not mine, honey," Corey said.

"Really?" Max leaned forward. "I found one in your locker. There was a note in it from Skylar saying 'He wants a bigger cut.' You expect me to believe you don't know anything about any of this?"

"I swear. I haven't lied to you about the rest of this, why would I start now?" Corey asked.

"You've done nothing *but* lie to me about this," Max said.

"I prevaricated. You didn't know everything, but I didn't outright lie to you. There's a difference." The smug smile returned.

"As far as who 'he' is, I have no idea. Obviously it was his source, but, again, I don't know who it was."

"Fine. It stops. Now. Today." Max leaned back in his chair. "I'm still trying to decide if I'm going to fire you."

Corey stared at Max. The disbelief on his face could have been wiped off with a dry cloth. "You're…kidding, right?"

"Maybe *you* don't know *me*," Max said. He took a deep breath and blew it out slowly. "Corey, I'm probably the biggest moron in the world right now, but I honestly do *not* want to fire you. I want answers, but I don't think you can give them to me. Not unless Skylar let you in on who his source was."

Corey shook his head.

"I thought not. Do you know anyone here at the gym who he dealt to?" Max asked.

"A few, yes, but I doubt you'll get them to admit to it."

"I don't really need them to admit it," Max said. "I just want to see if they know who Skylar's source was." Max sat quietly for a few minutes, running plans through his head. "Are you willing to help me?"

Corey stared back at him. "Are you sure you can trust me?"

"Well, not when you ask questions like that," Max said. "Honestly, Corey, was this about the money, or was it just some thrill you got involved in when you started sleeping with Skylar?"

"A little bit of both," Corey admitted. "My life needed something to pep it up. Skylar gave that to me on different fronts. However, everyone needs money, Max. I make pretty decent wages, but I'm single, and trying to live before I die. That isn't cheap. You would know that if you hadn't been born with a stick up your butt."

"You just don't know when to shut your mouth, do you?" Max asked. "I'm serious—well, I'm trying to be. You just won't cooperate."

"I need more money," Corey said. "There. Are you happy?"

"No. I would be if you'd drop the pretty, pretty princess act and attempt to be a decent human being for once," Max spat.

"Retract your claws, kitty. They're cutting pretty deep. This goes back to you not knowing me," Corey said.

"Let me in, then."

Corey shook his head. "Not now. Maybe not ever. I'm sorry, but that's just the way it is. The best thing you can do is quit treating me like a flaming queen and treat me like a person."

"You *are* a flaming queen."

"With feelings, Max, with feelings. I didn't stomp on your heart when Bobby dumped you, even though you've walked all over me pretty much from the beginning." Corey stood up and leaned across the desk. He glared at Max. "I'll help you however I can. I want to know who killed Skylar as much as you do. I know it's not Bobby. He's too sweet to do that. But I will not lift one finger if you don't change how you treat me."

"Fine," Max said gruffly. He took another deep breath. "I'm sorry. Fine, I'll change. However, I want you to stop pushing steroids or *any* kind of drugs in the gym. If I find out you haven't, you're gone. Deal?"

"Kiss on it?" Corey grinned.

"Going once" Max said.

"Fine. Deal. I promise no more drugs of any kind. The metaphorical juice bar is closed," Corey said. "So, where do we start?"

"I have no idea," Max said. "I'll let you know. In the meantime, can you give me a list of names for Skylar's buyers?"

"All the ones I know," Corey said.

Chapter Twenty-Four

"You're walking along a beach. You feel the gentle breeze blowing through your hair as the warm rays of the sun fill you with a sense of calm." Eden turned the volume down just as a sea gull screeched. The sound of crashing waves filled her office. "Let the sand squish up between your toes. You look off into the distance. What do you see?"

I see myself sitting in your office, pretending I'm not crazy. "Um, a lighthouse?"

"That's good," she said. "Now, I want you to focus on it and describe it to me—every detail you can imagine."

"It's tall...and white. A blue stripe winds around it from the base to the top." *How do I get talked into this crap? I just wanted the dog book back.*

"Keep going," she urged. "You're getting closer to it. What other details can you see? Sounds? Smells?"

"Smells? Really?"

"You're not focusing," she chided in a sing-song voice.

"Right. Um, the light isn't on because it's a beautiful day. A bird is circling around the top. It's looking down at me and screeching." He licked his lips and scrunched his eyes shut tighter. "There's, um, a man. A man is leaning over the railing at the top. He sees me and smiles."

"It's that lovely Detective Harris," Eden encouraged.

Max smiled and felt heat slowly rising in his face and ears. "Yeah, it's William," he admits. "He's so handsome, and that body of his—it's to die for."

"Reel it back in. This is mediation not fantasy porn."

He scowled. "Hey, if it helps me relax, what does it matter?"

"To you? Nothing. To me, well, let's just say I don't need to hear about hot men I can't have." She pulled her hands from his and placed them on either side of his head. "Now, we know it's William. What is he doing other than looking terribly attractive?"

"He's just staring out at the ocean." *So I guess I've got it bad for him when I see him while meditating.* "Are we finished? I don't think this is working."

Eden had started humming while massaging the sides of his head. "Stay focused for a few more minutes," she said before resuming the humming.

When her hands moved away, Max barely opened his eyes. She picked up a silver rod and moved it around the edge of a small metal bowl sitting between him and her. It began to resonate and slowly built up to an almost unbearable pitch. She stopped when he clapped his hands over his ears.

"You're not relaxing."

"What do you expect with that nerve-wracking noise?" he asked. "That has to be the worst sound I've ever heard."

"It's a meditation bowl," she said.

"It's a torture device," he shot back. The look of hurt on her face stabbed his heart. "I'm sorry. It doesn't help *me* relax, but I'm sure it's a lovely thing." He stood up and stretched his legs.

"The bowl is apparently not for everyone." She shoved it into a purple velvet bag and set it on the desk with a little less force than was necessary to splinter the wood. "You're book is on the shelf. Don't forget it this time, please."

Great, now I've hurt her feelings. I think I'll just make my way down the list of friends I have and alienate them one by one. "Eden, I'm sorry. Please, forgive me. I didn't mean it." He placed his hand on her shoulder. "You don't deserve me being so crass."

"No, I do not." She stood with her back to him for a long time without acknowledging him. Her shoulders rose and feel with the rhythmic breathing she was apparently forcing herself to do. After an eternity, she turned around. Her smile was a few teeth short of sincere. "You should be going, Max. It's late, and I know you want to meet Kandy for supper."

"Not until you say you forgive me," he said.

"That's the thing. I always forgive. Resentment and hard feelings do nothing but block your chakras. They cut you off from the mystic energy of the universe." She closed her eyes and lifted her hands toward the ceiling. "I prefer to have a clean aura. I wish I could convince you to do the same."

"Hello? Is anyone there?" a sweet voice called from the show room.

"I'll be right out, Henny," Eden said. "Have a good night, Max." She patted his cheek lovingly on her way out the door.

Max followed her and greeted Henrietta with a smile. It fell away when he saw the look on her face. "What's wrong?"

"You should be nicer to dear, sweet Eden," the older woman said. "She just wants to help you."

Max looked at Eden. "You've already told her?"

"I said nothing," Eden promised.

"Oh, you know my darlings listen to everything," Henny said. "Seriously, Max, we understand your situation, and we do try our best to help. It wouldn't hurt you to let us."

"My sentiments exactly," Eden said. She clasped Henny's hands in her own. Tears threatened at the corners of her eyes.

I can't win. When is the giant meteor just going to pummel me into the ground? "I'm sorry. Both of you please believe me."

"Actions speak louder than words, dear," Henny said.

Max sighed. "Of course. I'll do better." *I've got to get away from here. Maybe I could go back to Barbados. Maybe I* should!

"You could also do nicer by that dear Corey. 'Pretty, pretty princess,' is that what you called him?" Henny clucked her tongue and shook her head. "You boys shouldn't be so mean to each other."

She must be in tight with the NSA, or the aliens that have obviously abducted me and scooped out my brain. He stared at her for a few seconds, not knowing what to say. "Um, Kandy's waiting for me."

They're both so crazy they've synced up. He grabbed his coat from the counter and pulled it on, buttoning it before he stepped outside. A light snow had started, which was a pleasant change from the deluge of freezing rain that usually covered everything in ice.

He heard voices and turned to see Jamie and Elaine walking through the parking lot from their store. She turned and smiled at Max, but Jamie remained face-forward, marching toward his truck. Max waved; Elaine jogged over to him.

"Hey, Max, I'm sorry Jaime is still being a butt. I tell you that man is so stubborn sometimes," she said.

"Don't worry about it," he said. "I'm sure he'll come around when he's ready. Apparently I'm just ruining everyone's days around here."

She hugged him quickly before casting an ugly look at her husband, who was sitting in the truck, honking his horn impatiently. "Well, we're off to get some dinner before we come back and do some inventory. Can we bring you anything?"

"No, thank you," he said. "I'm on my way to eat with Kandy. You have a good time."

She thanked him and hurried to the truck. As they pulled out of the parking lot, Jamie's hand appeared from his window, his middle finger clearly intended for Max.

Max shook his head and turned toward Mind Your Own Beans. He stopped short when he almost ran into Henrietta. *What is this—random encounter time?*

"That young man is just a rascal," Henny said. She *tsk*-ed a couple times. "Max, dear, I'm truly sorry if I offended you. Sometimes I jump on a bandwagon and don't know when to jump back off. Can you forgive me?"

Max laughed softly. "Henny, I've upset so many people over the past couple days. I've apologized—or attempted to—so much. Jamie is mad at me, as you saw, and Eden's feelings are hurt. Corey...well, Corey is something else entirely, but I think I've managed to sort things out with him and establish a weird, workable arrangement for the time being."

She wrapped her arm in his, and they walked along the sidewalk. The snowflakes had grown in size, resembling feathers plucked from a duck's belly. Henny moved closer to him.

"We all make fools of ourselves. Sometimes we hurt those we care most about," she said. "It's a nasty business that's been going on around here. My darlings can barely keep up with all of it."

"Do your darlings tell you everything?" He felt ridiculous asking the question, but maybe in some odd twist of fate, Henrietta Gallowylde was the sane, normal one, and everyone else was eccentric.

"Oh, they tell me what they think I should know," she said.

"How do *they* know? They seem very well informed," he said.

"Well, dear, they are fairies after all." She said it like it was the most evident truth of the universe. "You sure do seem so fascinated by my darlings. Every time we're together you bring them up. Why is that, dear?"

"Because I *am* fascinated by them, and the information they come by. They don't happen to know more about this situation with Skylar and Corey, do they?" He didn't want to divulge the fact that drugs had been sold in the gym, and he was curious if Henny knew anything about what seemed to be a well-kept secret.

"They're very cautious boys," she said. "Just because I know things doesn't mean that I always tell them, either. People should be entitled to their privacy, dear."

They stopped in front of Crumbles just as John was locking the door. "Hey, Max, is she bothering you?"

"She's never a bother." Max patted her hand. "Well, you two have a good night. Henny, if you do decide there is anything you can tell me, please do."

"Of course, dear." She released his arm and traded it for her husband's. Together they walked to their car.

The warmth and smells of the coffee shop wrapped their arms around Max as soon as he opened the door and pulled him inside. He shook the snow from his coat when he removed it and tossed it onto the back of a chair.

A few customers lingered over their cups, but true to form, Kandy did nothing but make them feel comfortable and welcome. She stopped at his table long enough to pour a cup of coffee for him before disappearing into the back.

After everyone had left and the door was locked, Kandy set a plate in front of him and melted into the chair opposite. "What a crazy day," she sighed. "But at least it's over."

"Small miracles," he said. "You look beat. Is it time to hire some seasonal help yet?"

"I should have already done it, but you know me."

"Yes, I do." He took a bite of the sandwich, followed by a sip of coffee. "Do you think you'll actually hire someone this year or just kick yourself for not doing it—again?"

"I see you're still making friends and influencing people," she said with a mischievous grin.

He groaned. "Good news travels fast."

"Not as fast as Corey's mouth." She stopped short. "I hope you know what I mean by that because—*eww*."

"I understood." He laughed. "Yeah, I'm Mr. Congeniality today, but can we not talk about that? I've covered it with everyone else, and I just want to enjoy your company and your food."

"I think I can live with that," she said. "So, Corey's been selling steroids?"

He choked on coffee and pressed a napkin to his mouth to keep from spitting it everywhere. "He told you that?"

"Corey. Mouth. I believe we just covered that topic," she said.

"He wasn't supposed to tell anyone."

"Well, as far as I know, he's only told me, but you may want to make sure the hatch on his mouth gets sealed better. If that's possible," she added.

Before Max could respond, his phone rang. "Well, speak of the devil." He held his phone up so Kandy could see the caller ID with Corey's name. "Hello?"

Silence greeted him on the other end.

"Corey? Are you there?"

A sound like wet paper ripping came through the phone, and then Corey said, "*Help.*"

The phone went dead.

Chapter Twenty-Five

"Call 911," Max said. "Police and ambulance." He left his coat behind and sprinted to the door, slamming into it before he remembered Kandy had locked it. Once through, he raced down the sidewalk toward the gym. *Please be alright. Please be alright.*

He rounded the slight corner that separated Tight/Fit from The Vapor Trail. One of the windows had been shattered, and since it went from the ground to near the roof, glass littered the area, inside and out. Max dashed through the jagged-edged opening.

"Corey!" He ran from the reception area down the hall to the juice bar to the free weights room to the aerobics area, constantly shouting. He ran past the saunas toward the locker room.

Hands in front of himself, he ran into the door, immediately cursing and wringing his hands when his wrists bent back. The door was firmly stuck. He didn't bother with a second attempt. Rounding the corner into the next hallway, he saw the second door ajar.

"Corey!" He kneeled beside the lithe man. A small pool of blood was forming under Corey, and his breathing sounded like a water hose set at a slow trickle. His pulse was fading.

"Help! Somebody help!" He didn't know who he expected to hear him, but the feelings of helplessness were unbearable. Gently, he rolled Corey onto his back. The tear in his shirt near the center right of his chest neatly lined up with the puncture wound in his flesh. Max pressed his hand to it and shouted again.

"Max."

He almost didn't hear his name because it had been said so faintly. Unfortunately it hadn't been Corey who said it. From farther down the hall, Zane Rogers stumbled toward him. The owner of My

Parents' Basement was pressing his hand to the back of his head. He stopped briefly to throw up before continuing onward.

"Zane, Corey's dying. What happened?" Max hated how his voice cracked, and he dashed away tears with the heel of his hand.

"I heard the glass break and came to find out what was going on. Someone hit me from behind. I had no idea Corey was even in here." Zane kneeled, looking over Corey's wounded body.

Max used his free hand to steady his wobbly helper. The wail of sirens slowly reached his ears. "Thank God. Stay with me, Corey," he whispered. "Are you going to be okay if I go lead the paramedics back here?"

Zane nodded and almost went to the floor. "Bad idea. Go. I'll stay with him."

"Max? Max, are you in here?"

"Kandy, I'm coming," he shouted. He ran to her, and noticed she still had her phone clutched in her hand.

"My God! Max, are you hurt?" She grabbed his face and started turning him around, looking for the source of the blood covering his legs and hands.

"I'm fine. It's Corey." An ambulance and a police car screeched to a stop in the crunchy snow in front of the door. "Over here. Hurry! Someone's been stabbed."

Max led them through the gym to Corey. Zane leaned against the wall, throwing up again. Kandy comforted him while the paramedics tended to Corey.

Within minutes police had swarmed over the entire gym. A second ambulance arrived just as the first one left with Corey. *St. Francis is close. They'll get him there in time. They have to.*

"Max."

So many people calling my name. He slid down the wall, dipping his head between his knees. Tears dripped from his cheeks and the end of his nose.

"Max." A strong hand rested on the back of his, tenderly rubbing in circles. "Are you okay?"

He looked up into the concerned eyes of Detective Harris. "They got Corey. And Zane."

"I know," Harris said. "I thought it was you. I thought it was you," he whispered while pulling Max into a tight hug.

"Blood. Your suit." Max tried to pull away but his own strength was giving out, and Harris's was fueled by fear and relief.

"Hush. Just let me hold you." Harris rocked him back and forth.

Someone overhead cleared his throat. "Um, Detective, I'm sorry to disturb you, but you're going to want to see this."

"I'll be right back," Harris promised.

"I've got him until you do," Kandy said. She handed tissue to Max and squeezed Harris's arm as he walked past.

Max sat quietly staring at his blood-red hands. The tissue's stark white in relief against the tinted flesh mesmerized him. "So much."

"Just rest. Breathe and relax, Max," Kandy coaxed. "Are you cold? I can find you a blanket or something."

He looked at her. "Cold? No, I'm not cold. I'm shocked but I don't think I'm *in* shock. Thanks." He looked at her pants. "You've got blood and vomit on you."

"I know. So do you." She grabbed his chin before he could look down at himself.

His words were interrupted by someone banging on the door that let into the alley. The person's shouts were indiscernible through the steel. An officer fumbled with the lock before he managed to get it opened.

"Two more out here," a policeman outside said. He brushed snow from his mustache. "Man and woman. They're both alive, but he got banged up. Ambulance is on the way."

Max pushed himself to his feet and stumbled to the door.

"Whoa, sir, I'm going to need you to stay inside," the officer without the mustache told him.

"But who is it?" He pulled his hand out of Kandy's grasp, waving off her attempts to get him to sit back down.

"It's okay, guys." Harris stepped up to them and took Max by the arm. "He's with me. Let us through."

"Yes, sir," they both said in unison and stepped out of the way.

To his left, Max saw only the dumpster, but to the right he saw a few more officers helping Elaine Robertson stand up. She had a gauze pad clamped over her forearm, and a woman was holding another pad to Elaine's forehead. Jaime was lying on the ground, clearly unconscious. A red line trickled across his face.

Max locked eyes with Elaine. Walking with Harris to her, he asked, "Are you alright? Considering, I know."

"They say we'll be okay," she said. She looked down. "My boots. I bled on them."

"How did you manage to get attacked? And out here?" Harris asked.

"I forgot my purse and had to come back for it. We saw someone running away from the gym," she said. "When he saw us, he turned and ran down the alley. Jaime chased him. I heard them fighting, and when I got back here, Jamie was on the ground. The man attacked me, and I fell and hit my head when he cut me with the knife."

"Did you get a look at him? Anyone you know?" Harris asked.

She shook her head. "He had on a black ski mask. I'm afraid I'm not going to be much help."

"Thanks, Elaine. I'm so sorry you got pulled into this mess," Max said. He turned back toward the steel door.

"It's not your fault, Max. There are some things even you can't control or change," Elaine said.

"Come on, you're going to freeze," Harris said.

"If I get cleaned up, can you take me to the hospital?" Max asked.

"It's going to be a while," Harris said. "Kandy will be able to take you faster than I can."

Max nodded. They stopped inside the door, and Harris rubbed Max's arms. "Can I grab some clothes from my locker?"

"No," Harris said.

"Can you get them for me?"

Harris shook his head. "I can't do that either." He pulled Max back to the door where Corey had lain and pushed it open.

"What?" Max couldn't figure out what was going on. He looked at the floor, but Harris lifted his chin so he could look into the locker room.

Max gasped. It looked like a bomb had exploded. Locker doors had been forced open and entire sections had been toppled over. The floor was awash in clothing and debris. He looked at the other door and saw a stack of lockers slanted against it.

"Well, I know why Corey was targeted," he said.

"I think we all do," Harris said.

Chapter Twenty-Six

Max took a drink of his coffee and grimaced at the taste of the unexpectedly cold liquid. *How long have I just been sitting here?*

He and Harris had spent most of the previous night either at St. Francis, waiting for Corey to make it out of surgery, or holding down the fort at the gym while a repair crew covered the cavernous missing window with plywood. He hadn't found the strength to go back to the locker room.

He was still amazed at how quickly the police actually released a crime scene. *Nothing like the movies.* After a few hours, they were gone. Luckily Harris had hired an off-duty policeman to run security while they were at the hospital.

Max had wanted to send the man home when they got back at two o'clock in the morning, but Harris had convinced him to let go of that.

"I've already paid him for the night, and he doesn't work tomorrow. If nothing else, you can think of it as helping give his kids a better Christmas," Harris said.

"Will do," Max said. "Thank you for being here. I'm sure you're exhausted. Do you work tomorrow?"

"I do, but don't worry about me," Harris said. "I've done this countless times. Once more isn't going to hurt, especially since I'm doing it for you."

"Are you out at work?" Max had no idea why the question was suddenly so important. *Well, yes I do.* "Are you going to get into trouble for hugging me earlier? It doesn't take a detective to realize you have feelings for me."

"I am. I catch hell for it from some, but others don't care," Harris said. "Police are supposed to be macho, manly men, and for some reason, people think gay guys aren't either of the three. I've proven more than enough of them wrong on that count.

"As for the hug, only one of the officers saw that, and he's a friend. He won't tell anyone. I promise," Harris said.

"I just don't want to be the cause for you catching flack," Max said. He pulled Harris closer, resting his head on the man's shoulder. The faint smell of aftershave tickled his nose.

"I'm fine. I promise. Let's worry about getting this place back in shape," Harris said. "I'm going to run to Quik Trip and get some coffee. Do you want some?"

"Please. Don't forget to see if Officer Yarborough wants some, too."

"I'll be back in few. Try to rest while I'm gone," Harris said.

That was…five hours ago. No wonder this is cold. He carried the cup to the juice bar and dumped it into the sink. After he tossed the cup into the trash, he looked around. Even knowing Corey had come through surgery without complications, he still felt a sense of loss. *This room feels like a tomb, now. Probably will until he gets back.*

He wiped away tears. *Time to stop that crap.* He breathed deeply and slowly released it. His phone ringing scared him, and he fumbled it from his pocket.

"Hello."

"Yeah, this is Dave with the crime scene clean-up. I was just making sure someone would be there to let us in. We'll be there in about thirty minutes."

"I'm here. Come when you're ready." He ended the call. *Maybe I should go have a look around first.* He knew they would just clean up the blood, and the police had been over every inch of the locker room. It just felt necessary to give it a look. *Even if a lot of Corey's blood is on the floor.*

Thankfully, a few of the policemen had moved the lockers blocking the second entrance, so Max went through it to avoid the congealed mess. He propped the door open and imagined he stood at the precipice of the abyss. The detritus of a gym society stretched out before him, leading into the apocalyptic wasteland of the showers beyond.

Not enough coffee. Or sleep. This isn't Mad Max. He chuckled softly and scrubbed his face. *I should shave.*

He stepped inside and nearly slipped on a duffel bag. *I'm going to have to sort all this out and let people claim their stuff. How long am I going to have the gym closed for this? God, Elizabeth Walker will flay me alive.*

Stepping cautiously over or around the mess, he worked on righting the sections of toppled lockers. It was back-breaking work, but it gave him something to focus on other than the metallic scent in the air. Before long, he heard Officer Yarborough calling out to him, and went to meet the man at the front.

"Here's the clean-up crew, Mr. Cantor," he said. "If you don't mind, I'm going to head out and get some rest. Detective Harris said to tell you to do the same. If you want, we have another buddy who can keep an eye on things for you until that happens."

"Thank you, but I have someone coming today to replace the window. I appreciate your help. Have a Merry Christmas." Max shook the officer's hand and turned to the newly arrived group. "Dave?"

"That's me," said one of the guys in a yellow haz-mat suit. "If you'll show us where to go, we'll get started. This shouldn't take any time at all, from what Detective Harris said."

Max led them to the site and re-entered the locker room. He didn't find much that was covered in blood. Apparently, whoever had stabbed Corey had attacked him right at the door—most likely when Corey walked in on him.

He had so many questions that couldn't be answered until Corey recovered. Why had Corey come back after leaving for the day? Why hadn't he called the police when he saw the broken window and heard the obvious commotion going on in the locker room?

Max stopped in the middle of picking up several towels from the floor. *What if Corey did this? But who stabbed him? Did he have a helper that decided to double cross him?* He dropped the towels back on the floor and sank onto one of the benches. *Maybe I'm just being paranoid with all that's happened involving Corey. Surely he wouldn't do this.*

"Would he?" Max whispered.

A knock on the door behind him startled Max from his dark thoughts. "Zane. Hey, I'm glad to see you. How's your noggin?" He made his way over to his friend, who had gauze wrapped around his head.

"The doctor says I'll be fine. I just got a really bad knock and a pretty decent concussion, but otherwise no big deal." Zane handed him a cup of coffee. "Kandy thought you might need this. She says when her temp gets in she'll bring you something to eat."

"Thank you." Max sipped the hot liquid, thankful for the jolt of caffeine. "Let's go sit down. I want to ask you some questions, if you have time."

"Sure," Zane said. "Jo's over at the store. She'll be able to manage until I get back. Not too many nerds beating down the doors today since it's not Wednesday."

"Wednesday?" Max asked.

"New comics day." Zane chuckled. "I have to admit I'm one of the worst, though. Every Wednesday is like Christmas when you're a comic-book-loving geek."

Max smiled. They sat in a couple chairs outside the sauna area. They were the closest chairs, but Max regretted the decision when his eyes latched onto the door to the sauna. *This place is becoming one bad memory after another.*

"So, what do you want to know?" Zane asked.

Max took a drink. "Did you hear Corey talking to anyone when you got close to the locker room?"

"No," Zane said. "I didn't hear anything. I was coming down the outer hallway. Whoever whacked me in the head had probably already stabbed Corey. Not sure why they attacked me, but I'm thankful I didn't get stabbed."

"They?"

"Well, I don't know if it was a man or woman. I don't even know how many people were in here," Zane said. "I just remember walking and then waking up when I heard you screaming for help. I'm afraid I'm not going to be a very useful source of information."

"It's okay," Max said, even though he felt his frustration rising. *Why can't I get a break with all this?* "If you think of anything else, would you let me know?"

"Sure thing." Zane stood up and stretched out his long legs. "So, Jo and I were wondering if you and Detective Harris would like to get together for dinner sometime. He seems like a really nice guy, and we'd like to get to know him better."

"Thanks, Zane, but we're not together." Max stood up. "It'll probably be a while, but I definitely want to do it. It's been too long."

"Tell me about it." Zane shook his hand, said goodbye, and left.

Max turned back toward the locker room, but his phone started ringing. He pulled it from his pocket and groaned.

The caller ID showed Jamie Robertson.

Chapter Twenty-Seven

What gay hell is this?

"Um, hello," Max said after swiping the green "receive" icon on the screen.

"Hey, partner, it's Jamie," he said. *"Listen, um, I was wondering if you might come over to the store when you get a chance. There's something, um, I want to talk to you about. If that's okay?"*

No! "Sure. What's a good time for you?" Max asked.

"No hurry. I know you have your hands full over there," Jamie said. *"Just whenever you get a chance. I'll be here all day."*

"No problem. I'll be over shortly."

"Thanks. Bye, Max." Jamie ended the call.

Max put the phone in his pocket and walked back to the locker room. *He better be willing to apologize, or else I'm done with him.*

His conscience stabbed at him, reminding him Jamie *had* been hurt trying to apprehend Corey's attacker. He wanted to feel bad, but after the verbal assault in Mind Your Own Beans, he had difficulty giving Jamie any slack. *We'll just see how it goes.*

He stopped in the doorway, looking in at the mess. It seemed almost insurmountable for some reason. *Maybe I just need to get some help. I'm sure Kandy or William won't mind pitching in. I just don't want to face this alone.*

He walked around the corner to the crew. "Hey, Dave, I'm going to be in my office if you need me."

"Sure thing, Mr. Cantor," Dave said. "We shouldn't be too much longer. This was a pretty basic job."

Max thanked him and walked away. He hated that Corey's near-death had been boiled down to a job to someone. The chair in his office welcomed him like a long-lost lover, and he felt the exhaustion catch up to him within seconds. He finished the last of the coffee Zane had brought for him then placed the cup on his desk next to his phone.

Jamie. God, I don't want to go over there. But I have to. He closed his eyes and leaned back in the chair.

"Mr. Cantor. Mr. Cantor, we're finished."

Max opened his eyes and looked at Dave standing in the doorway. He felt something wet on the side of his face and wiped at it with his fingers. *Drool. I was sleeping and drooling. Just great.*

"Hey, thanks, I appreciate all of your work," Max said, trying not to be embarrassed. "Do you bill me, or can I pay you now?"

"No need for money," Dave assured him. "This was a favor to Detective Harris. I owed him one for helping my son. Have a good day, Mr. Cantor."

"You, too." *William, you sweet, sweet man, I'm going to kick your butt.* He could imagine Harris's handsome smile and deep laughter. *There's a keeper.*

Max's phone indicated he had received a text message—William. *His ears must have been burning.* He responded with thanks and insistence on paying back what it had cost to have Dave come in.

Harris said, *'I'll think of some way. Eventually ;)'*

Max laughed. *'I'm sure you will,'* he responded. *'Going to go talk to Jamie. Wish me luck'.*

'Sure that's wise?'

'No. Going anyway. Have a good day. I love you.'

He hit "send" before he realized what the last sentence said. There was no way to take it back.

'Um, wow. Okay. Lots to talk about,' Harris responded.

Max groaned and sank into his chair. *'That's not how I wanted to say it,'* he sent back.

'☺ It's okay. Just unexpected. Well, not really. Talk later. Dinner, your choice.'

Max set the phone back down and sighed contentedly. "This is so crazy," he said to no one. "Willie Harris, of all people." He laughed and scrubbed the sleep from his eyes. Then he remembered Jamie. *Time to get it over with.*

He went to the restroom, splashed water on his face, and combed his wet fingers through his hair. The light purple under his eyes elicited a groan, but he shook it off. That was to be expected after yesterday.

The short walk to The Vapor Trail chilled his face almost to numbness. The wind was biting and bitter, tossing up tiny bits of frozen snow and blowing it around like knives in a blender. He rushed into the warm, inviting comfort of the Robertsons' store and leaned against the door.

"Winter in Oklahoma—nothing like it to make you realize how stupid you are for living here, huh?" Jamie chuckled from behind the counter. "Thanks for coming, Max."

Max nodded while removing his coat and shaking off Mother Nature's dandruff. "What's up?" he asked. He forced eye contact even though he didn't truly want to look at the man.

"How's Corey doing?" Jamie asked.

"Fine. Why did you call me over here? I've got a lot to do," Max said. He let his tone become gruffer than he felt.

Jamie licked his lips and rubbed at the gauze pad taped to his forehead. "I, um, I just wanted to say…Well, you know, partner. I'm sorry for being such a jerk the other day," he spat out in a rush.

"You mean when you called me a fag?" Max asked. *You're not getting off this easily.*

Jamie turned red and lowered his eyes. "Um, yeah, that. I was mad, and I shouldn't have said it."

"It's what you feel and think, though, isn't it?" Max asked. "Skylar, Corey, Bobby, William, me—we're all just a bunch of fags to you, aren't we? We don't deserve respect as humans because we're just a bunch of *fags.* Right?"

Jamie's head was so far down only the top of it could be seen. Max felt the anger coursing through his veins like wildfire. He hadn't intended to be this confrontational, but everything snowballed into this one outlet so conveniently in front of him.

"I'm sorry," Jamie said. He slowly lifted his head, and Max could tell the man didn't want to look directly at him but was forcing it.

We're not so different. The thought angered him more.

"I've apologized to John and Kandy," Jamie said, "but I didn't know how to truly apologize to you. I knew I had hurt you very badly. Honestly, that's why I said it in the first place. I wanted to hurt you because you accused me of killing Skylar. It hurt that you thought I could be capable of that."

"You're a homophobe, Jamie," Max said. "You want to throw the word 'fag' around like it's no big deal. But it is a big deal. To a lot of people it's the last thing they hear before their family cuts them off or before they get beaten to death."

"I know, and I promise to change. I just need you to forgive me. Please."

Max's shoulders slowly sagged. He didn't know if he could find the words or the sentiment to accept the apology. Finally, he settled for asking, "How's Elaine?"

"She's pretty shook up," Jamie said. If he was upset Max hadn't forgiven him, he didn't show it. "She decided to stay at home today. We didn't get much sleep last night after I got out of the hospital. That fella did a number on us."

"I'm glad neither one of you were hurt too badly," Max said. "Do you remember anything about what happened?"

Jamie shook his head. "No. Doc says I probably won't, either. I remember getting out of the truck, but everything after that is a blank. Good thing I have a thick skull, I guess." He smiled sheepishly at his self-deprecating jab.

Max decided to take the bait as a show of the peace process started. "Yeah, probably so." He placed his hands on the counter and stared at Jamie long enough for the man to start squirming. "If you ever say that word again where I can hear it, you better pray someone can drag me off you. Get me?"

"I do, partner. I do." Jamie held out his hand. "No more of the bad word. I promise."

Max gave him a single, resolute nod and shook his hand. "So, it's getting close to lunch time. Do you want me to hang out here while you take Elaine something to eat?"

"Um, sure," Jamie said. "I don't think you'll get too busy, and if you have any questions, you can just call me. I really appreciate the offer, Max."

"You're welcome. Tell Elaine I hope she's back soon, and thank you—both—for trying to look out for me." Max stole Jamie's signature move and clapped the man on the back. "You're a decent person when you're not showing your butt."

"Thanks," Jamie said. He grabbed his coat from a hook on the wall and pulled it on. "I'll be back as soon as possible."

"Take your time," Max said.

After Jamie left, Max sat in a chair and pulled out his phone. He checked his Facebook and Twitter feeds. When the bell at the front door chimed, he looked up. A scrawny guy dressed in coveralls stained with oil sauntered up to the counter.

"Hi, can I help you?" Max asked.

"Jamie here?"

"No, he stepped out for a few minutes. Is there something I can help you with?" Max offered.

"Name's Kyle. I'm here for my usual."

Max stared at him briefly. "I, uh, don't actually work here. I'm just covering for a few minutes. What's your usual, and where can I find it?"

Kyle walked back toward the entrance and pulled a bottle of amber-colored liquid from a shelf. He placed it on the counter then pointed at a brown box sitting on the floor near the emergency rear exit.

"Other stuff's in there. Just one," he said. He put a hundred dollar bill on the counter.

Max walked over to the box, kneeled down, and opened it. Inside were several bottles of clear liquid.

Chapter Twenty-Eight

"How much is it for both bottles?" Max asked.

"The hundred usually covers it," Kyle said. "Unless he's raised his prices again, that is. He tends to do that every once in a while."

"Well, if a hundred isn't enough, I'll cover the rest. Have a good day," Max said.

Kyle dipped his head and left the store.

Max went back to the box, pulling out bottle after bottle of the clear liquid. *Is this steroids or something else?* He unscrewed the lid and smelled. *Marijuana. This must be what Corey was talking about. Skylar found a way to smoke it through the modified e-cig. Jamie must have been helping him distribute it.*

He put all but one of the bottles back. That one he put into his pocket. *What else is going on around here?* He started going through the other boxes. Two of them contained bottles similar to the first one. The rest were filled with amber liquid.

Once everything was back where it belonged, he stepped into the tiny, cluttered office adjoining the point-of-sale area. Boxes were stacked from floor to ceiling, all of them labeled with various name and flavor combinations of nicotine liquids or vaping devices.

What am I looking for? He looked around the room, taking in the boxes, the clutter, the tiny desk. Opening one of the drawers of the desk, he found invoices and the FastSheet he compiled for the Robertsons every month. Nothing appeared out of the ordinary.

The drawer closed too loudly for his tastes, causing him to curse under his breath. *If I was Jamie, wanting to hide something, where would I put it?* He looked around some more. His thoughts raced, and he tried to mesh them with how he thought Jamie would think.

I'm arrogant and think I'm smarter and better than other people. I want to hide something from my wife without making her think I'm hiding it. Where?

Of course!

He pulled Jamie's gym bag from the bottom of a book shelf that held pictures of Jamie and Elaine from when they were dating up through last year's Christmas party. Noting how their smiles became smaller and less genuine in the successive photos, Max shook his head sadly.

Unzipping the bag, he attempted to go through the contents without disturbing them too much. The main compartment was filled with the usual gym accoutrements—clothes, towel, water bottle. In the side pouch he found a plastic case and a small black book. He removed them and was pressing the slide to open the container when the door chime sounded.

Adrenaline made him momentarily drunk while his mind decided what it was going to do—fight or flight. Reason reasserted itself quickly, and he re-zipped the pouch, dropped the bag back onto the shelf, and shoved the plastic case and book into the front of his jeans, tugging his shirt over it.

He moved back out into the point-of-sale area, looking for the person who had come in. "Henrietta, you scared me."

She cast a skeptical look at him. "Why on earth would my coming into the store frighten you, dear?" She looked around. "Where're Jamie and Elaine?"

"Elaine's home and Jamie took her something to eat. What can I do for you?" he asked. He hated how his voice wavered and warbled like a kid discovered with his hand in the cookie jar.

She eyed him a few moments more before saying, "My darlings told me something you might be interested in. There are some metal stones still left unturned."

"What? What does that mean?"

"I don't know, dear. They didn't tell me anything more than what I've told you." She moved around behind the counter and held the back of her hand to his forehead. "Max, are you feeling well? You look pale and clammy. I don't know if there's a bug going around, but you may have one."

"I'm fine," he said, hoping his voice sounded assuring. "It's just been a long twenty-four hours with little sleep and far too much adrenaline."

Henny clucked her tongue. "I know. Poor Corey. I seem to be saying that a lot."

"Yeah." Max stepped back and wrapped an arm around her shoulders to usher her to the door. "So, have you started making any of your fruitcake yet?"

She smiled and patted his cheek. "John says there's something wrong with the two of us." She made her voice as deep and gruff as it would go as she said, "'There's something not right with anyone who'll eat fruitcake.'"

"He just doesn't know what he's missing, especially from one of your fruitcakes. The best I've ever had. Just don't tell my grandmother I said that," he whispered.

"All of your secrets are safe with me," she laughed. "I'll have John bring you one in a few days."

"Thanks." He held the door open for her. "Do you want me to tell Jamie you stopped by?"

"No need, dear. He'll find out sooner or later. Bye." She pulled her coat tightly, shoving her hands under her arms, and hurried down the sidewalk.

Max allowed himself to breathe after the door was closed. *Fairy radar.* He walked back to the counter. The bell chimed again, and he turned around.

"Did you forget—Oh, hey, Jamie."

"Did I forget what?" Jamie brushed snow from his hair and pulled off his coat.

"Nothing," Max said. "Henny just left, and I thought maybe she was coming back to tell me something else weird and cryptic."

Jamie laughed. "I tell you, partner, that woman is spooky accurate with too much. If she does talk to fairies, we're all going to look like fools."

"I think I've said something similar," Max said. "Elaine doing okay?"

"Yeah, she's a tough old broad. She'll bounce back in no time. As a matter of fact she asked me to give you something." Jamie walked up and wrapped his arms around Max and kissed him quickly on the cheek.

"Um, okay. That was tender...and weird. Thanks. I think."

"Hey, she told me to do it. You really should shave, too." Jamie rubbed his lips with the back of his hand. "Feels like a porcupine."

Jamie hung his coat up and looked skeptically at the hundred dollar bill lying on the counter. "Is that yours, partner?"

"Oh, no, it's yours." *Let's see how he takes this.* "Somebody named Kyle came in after you left. He asked for something from that box by the door, and said the money should cover that bottle plus the other one he grabbed off a shelf."

"Yup, that covers it." Jamie pushed some buttons on the cash register and shoved the money into the drawer when it opened. "Thanks for your help. Let me know if I can return the favor."

He's not even batting an eye. "I will." Max's phone rang. "Sorry, it's William. I'll be right back." He walked toward the front of the store. "Hey, how's it going?"

"Fine. I'm sorry, but I can't make dinner tonight," William said. *"I've got a lead on a case, and I have to follow up on it. We'll have to try again tomorrow."*

"It's okay. I've got a few things to finish up around the gym, and then I'll be going home to sleep," Max said. "If you call, and I don't answer, it's because I'm passed out and sleeping like a stone."

"You need it," William said. *"By the way, I called St. Francis. Corey's still in ICU. No visitors, but the prognosis is improving. The doctor said he'll probably be in his own room by the end of the week."*

"I really should go see him," Max said.

"You need to rest first. Corey's in good hands."

"You're right. As usual," Max said.

"Well, I need to go. Have a good night."

"You, too." He ended the call.

"Well, looks like things are getting serious with the hot detective," Jamie said.

Max felt himself turning red. "What makes you say that?" he asked, walking back to Jamie.

"I just know the look. Used to see it every time I was in front of the mirror when Elaine and I were dating." Jamie clamped his mouth shut suddenly. He cleared his throat. "Well, anyway, I'm sure you want to get back to the gym and your clean up. Let me know if you want help."

Max saw hurt slowly working its way across Jamie's face. "You okay?"

"I'm fine, partner," Jamie said. He waved away the concern. "Things change. People change. Sometimes you can go back and recapture what you had. Sometimes you can't. Doesn't mean you don't try."

"Good luck, Jamie. I mean that."

"I know you do." Jamie turned away and walked to his office. He stopped at the door and grabbed onto the jamb. "If you and the detective do decide that you're 'together,' you take care of him, and make him take care of you. Don't ever give up what you know you want and deserve. No matter what anyone else tells you is right and wrong."

"Um, sure. Thanks." *If Oprah steps out of the shadows I'm going to freak.* "Have a good evening."

Jamie nodded and disappeared into the office. Max waited a few seconds then retrieved his coat and bundled up. Outside he took two steps toward the gym before turning around and walking the other way.

Chapter Twenty-Nine

"Creamy tomato-basil soup and a whole grilled three-cheese sandwich. Do you want any more coffee?" Kandy asked.

"I may need a ride home after this," Max responded. "All this comfort food after this day is putting me right to sleep."

She ruffled his hair. "Well, if you want, I can drive you, or I can follow you in my car to make sure you get there safely."

He nodded through a drink of coffee. "I'll take you up on one of those. Oh, and more would be great." He slid his cup toward the edge of the table.

"I live to serve." She gave his hair another tussle before leaving to retrieve more life-sustaining black gold.

Max groaned and pulled the liberated contents of Jamie's duffel bag from his pants. He'd forgotten to remove them before sitting down, and he didn't want to do it with Kandy standing over him. *I want to see if it's anything before I start bringing others into it.*

He left the items lying in his lap until Kandy had topped off his coffee and moved on to deal with the horde packed into the shop. It never ceased to amaze him how people, when it was blisteringly cold or snowing, seemed to flock to restaurants and businesses.

Glancing around to make sure no one paid attention to him, he slid the latch on the plastic case and slowly opened it. Inside he found a vaping device, a full bottle of clear liquid, and a nearly-empty bottle of amber liquid.

I know these things pretty much all look alike, but I swear that's the one Corey dropped. He removed the long black device and turned it over and over in an attempt to find any discernable markings. Unfortunately, he found none.

He started to close the lid when he noticed a scrap of paper under one of the bottles. The words "The good stuff" were printed onto the small white square.

I wonder which bottle it means. He replaced the contents and slipped the case into his coat. While finishing off the rest of his food, he opened the small black book and flattened it out on the table.

Between slurps of orange-red creamy deliciousness and bites of gooey, stringy warmth, he perused the lines of numbers written haphazardly in the spaces of the book. The handwriting obviously belonged to Skylar, but his abbreviated notes beside the number amounts were indiscernible to anyone but him.

Page after page, Max ran his finger and mind over the figures. *This is an accountant's nightmare, but I'm pretty sure small-time drug dealers aren't too concerned with good books.*

"What's that?" Kandy stepped up beside him, gently resting a hand on his shoulder. "That's a mess. I assume it's not yours."

"No," he said. "I'm going over it for a friend."

"Liar." Her tone wasn't accusatory, but he could tell she knew.

He looked around again before softly saying, "I'm pretty sure it belongs to Skylar."

"I thought it looked familiar," she said, sliding into the chair across from him. "I've never seen inside it, but he was in here plenty of times, scribbling in it."

"Well, not that I'm condoning it, but he was definitely making quite a profit from his little dealings." Max flipped to the dates that coincided with Skylar's time spent with Bobby. "Being in the gym definitely helped him, too. More clients and greater exposure exploded whatever account he had."

"Speaking of which, are there any account numbers in there?" she asked.

He flipped through several pages and checked the front and back covers. "Not that I can see. Apparently he was smart enough not to do that. Well, okay, maybe not." He tapped the bottom of a page. "It looks like this may be it. Wait a minute."

He reached into his back pocket to retrieve his wallet and removed a card from it. "This is an account with the bank Bobby and I use."

"Do you think you can get access to it?"

"Possibly, but only if I pretend to be Skylar," he said. "That could be tricky if the person I talk to knows he's dead, and that's if the cops haven't already found the account and frozen it. There are so many possibilities."

"Kandy, I need some more coffee, please," someone said from a nearby table.

She excused herself and walked away with the coffee carafe. He pushed his empty dishes to the center of the table and leaned back, studiously going over the numbers again.

His phone rang, and he fished it from his pocket, receiving the call without checking the caller ID. "Hello?"

"Hey, partner," Jamie said. "There's a lady hangin' out in front of the gym. Kinda tall, nice legs, several other assets that are nice to behold, too. Also looks like she could chew a metal fence post and spit out nails."

Elizabeth Walker. What did I do to deserve this woman? I'm in gay hell. "Thanks. I'll be right there."

"Leaving so soon?" Kandy asked from behind.

"Unfortunately, yes. I've got a core meltdown in progress at the gym, and even though I thought I had defused it a few days ago, I was apparently wrong." He pulled on his coat and tucked the small book into his back pocket with his wallet. "Wish me luck."

She hugged him. "Let me know when you're ready to go home. The offer still stands."

"Thanks."

The wind had died down, and the snow blanketing the parking lot reflected the abundance of sunlight like a billion crystals strewn along a waterless beach. *Too bad I can't just enjoy this. But, no, I have to go deal with Elizabeth Walker.*

As if thinking her name had conjured her into being, the woman stepped around the corner of Tight/Fit and stared at him. He took a deep breath and steeled himself for the tirade about to hit him like a nuclear blast's shockwave.

"Hello, Elizabeth," he said with the friendliest smile he could manage. "Look, I'm really sorry—"

She held up her hand. "It's okay, Max. I'm not here to work out. I actually just wanted to...talk."

He was shocked to realize she was smiling at him—warmly and like a friend would. "Um, wow, of-of course, Elizabeth." He fumbled his keys from his pocket and unlocked the door. "Come in to my office. Would you like anything to drink?"

"No, thank you." She preceded him into the building and waited patiently while he turned on a few lights and then showed her into his office.

What's going on? This is weird. He pointed at Bobby's chair and pulled his own around to the side of the desks so he could be closer to her. "So, what's on your mind?"

She looked around the room, and he realized she was uncomfortable and obviously stalling for time. "Well, I, um, wanted to apologize for being...well, I think we both know what I've been." She shrugged her shoulders in one of the most self-conscious, vulnerable displays he had ever seen from her.

"Oh, Elizabeth, here." He handed her a box of tissue when tears started running down her cheeks. "It's not that bad. I'm a big boy. Besides, I have to apologize for being a jackass, too. I've said—and thought—some really terrible things to and about you over the past couple weeks."

She wiped her nose and waved away his words. "Then we can forgive each other. I just needed to come tell you I was sorry, but also to tell you why I've been behaving this way." She took a deep breath, her shoulders thrown back, and when she released it, she looked half her usual size. "I've been dealing with the death of my husband."

"Oh, Elizabeth..." Words tripped over his lips and fell to the floor. He cleared his throat. "I didn't know. I'm so very sorry."

"Not many people do," she whispered. "I don't have many friends." That admission seemed to destroy her more than telling him about her husband. Her tears flowed anew, and she shakily plucked more tissue from the box.

Max had no idea what to say. He leaned back in his chair and cast about for the right words. "Do you have anyone for support? Family? People you can trust? Anyone?"

She shook her head. "Have you met me? I haven't been a pleasant person for a very long time, Max. This is the result of that. I know I shouldn't be here burdening you with this, but, honestly, you're the only person who has ever even attempted to be nice to me."

"What about work?" His teeth clicked together when he clamped his mouth shut. The harsh words she had spat into the phone when firing an underling a few days ago replayed in his ears. "Um, no, probably not."

"It's funny," she said with a chuckle that held no humor, "I run a syndicated advice column, and I don't even know what to do."

"What column?" he asked. *She gives people advice? Holy crap!*

"I'm Aunt Liz," she said.

"Really? I love that column," he said. "How on earth do you—" He felt heat creeping up from his neck as his face turned red. Shame burned him from the inside out.

"How do I give people friendly advice when I'm, well, let's say less than friendly?" She laughed. "That's what a lot of people wonder, I assure you. I wasn't always this way. Just so much has happened. More than you ever want to know."

She leaned toward him and locked eyes with his. "How do I get past this, Max? The heartache is unbearable. I feel dead inside."

His eyes widened. "Elizabeth, I'm not one to give anybody advice. With all the stuff going on around here, my own house is in enough disarray that I shouldn't be telling someone else how to clean hers up."

She slowly leaned back in her chair. "You're right. I'm sorry to bother you." Standing up quickly, she shoved her hands in her pocket and walked out of the office.

Max followed. "Please, don't go. I'm not saying I won't help." He grabbed her arm, just intent on getting her to stop, but she turned so quickly and embraced him so hard, he almost fell over from the force of her momentum. He sighed and patted her back as she shook with sobs that echoed from the walls.

After an eternity of minutes, she took a ragged breath and wiped at his shirt with wadded-up tissue. "Sorry."

"No need to apologize," he said. "If I'd had someone to do that with a few months ago, I wouldn't have spent two months drunk on a beach in Barbados. I could probably still use it."

She smiled at him. "My shoulder hasn't had snot on it for a while, but I'm pretty sure I remember how to be there for someone else—if you ever want to talk."

Max laughed. "Yeah, the big, brawny queen blubbering on Aunt Liz's shoulder—we could sell tickets and make a million."

"A Maximillian," she said. Her smile was truly genuine and reflected in her now-reddened eyes.

Max groaned. "And she's back, ladies and gentlemen." He hugged her again. "You going to be alright?"

"Eventually," she confessed. She started toward the door. "Thank you for letting me do this, Max. I can't truly express my gratitude."

"There's no need." He followed her outside and stood beside her while she stared across the parking lot.

"Max, there you are." Barry stopped next to him. "I'm sorry; I didn't realize you were busy. I can come back later." He turned to leave.

"No, it's okay," Max said. "Barry, have you ever met Elizabeth Walker?"

Barry's eyes immediately dropped toward the sidewalk. "I've watched, um, I mean I've seen, um, n-no, I haven't."

Max introduced them. "Elizabeth is having a pretty rough time right now. Oh, I hope you don't mind me saying that," Max said quickly, relieved when she shook her head. "Seeing you, I had a sudden thought that you might be in a unique situation to help set her up with someone to help cheer her up."

Barry stared at him, horrified, until realization spread across his face. "Yes. Yes! I think I could at that. Do you like dogs?" he asked her.

"Oh, well, I haven't had a dog in ages," she said. She cast a skeptical glance at Max.

"Barry runs Biscuit Acres, here in the mall, and he also helps with rescued animals. Not to mention he's a rather handsome devil," Max stage whispered.

Barry turned red. Elizabeth smiled. She stepped forward and wrapped her arm through Barry's. "I think a dog—and some handsome company—might do some wonders for me."

"Um, well, um, okay." Barry took a deep breath. "Come with me," he said.

Max watched them walk away and waved at Barry when the man briefly looked back. The smile on his face was priceless. He didn't move until they disappeared into Barry's store.

"This should be interesting," he said.

Chapter Thirty

Max stood inside the door, letting the warm-fuzzies flow through himself for a few minutes more before he sighed and leaned across the main reception counter. There was still so much to do, and his sleep-deprived brain was no help in focusing on what he needed to do next.

The locker room was still a war zone. Thankfully Corey's blood was just a very bad memory and not an actuality. *Why couldn't Dave clean up the rest, too?* He sighed again and walked—trudged—to the room in question.

Standing in the still-propped-open door, he stared at the mess for a few moments before clapping his hands and bouncing up and down a few times. "Let's get this done," he said to no one.

He retrieved several large trash bags from the nearby janitorial closet and made a quick initial sweep for gym-owned items that went into his "salvageable" or "non-salvageable" bags. It only took ten minutes to get through that task, and the sense of accomplishment revitalized him.

Next, he shoved personal items that belonged to gym members into the remaining bags. They filled up quickly, and he tied them off and set them beside the walls in the hallway. Finally, he saw the uncluttered floor and smiled.

Small victories, he thought. *I'll claim them where I can.*

The lockers has been placed more or less where they had initially been. He had nudged a couple stacks of them a few inches this way or that, but he had finally been satisfied they were where they needed to be. In all, only fifteen lockers had been pried open. The rest had had the locks cut off.

So, was this for drugs, or to take away something I hadn't found yet, or both? And what was Corey doing in here—catching someone in the act or receiving retribution from a hacked off dealer? He shook his head. *Only he can tell me, and I doubt that's going to happen. Oh well.*

He grabbed the two bags of trash he had filled up and went out to the dumpster through the exit. The door started closing when he was halfway through. Before he could stop it, a rough metallic edge dragged along his right arm leaving behind a stinging red line. The bag in that hand dropped to the snow-covered concrete, and he held up his arm to inspect it.

Not too bad. Hurts like hell. He retrieved the dropped garbage and headed for the dumpster. The sound of a door opening behind him caught his attention.

"Hey, partner, you still at it?" Jamie tossed a couple of containers into the snow before coming out carrying a large box full of smaller boxes.

"Almost finished," Max said. He tossed his bags into the open dumpster and went to collect the stuff Jamie had tossed out.

"Thanks, I appreciate the help," Jamie said. He dropped his burden into the huge waste container then relieved Max of one of his bags. Before he could toss it in, the bottom gave way, scattering the contents in a pile. "Well, crap!"

"That sucks. Here, let me help." Max kneeled down to assist with clean up. "Are these Elaine's?" He held up a pair of boots with dark stains on the toe and soles.

"Yeah, she bled on them and said she didn't want to try to clean them," Jamie said. "Guess they would just remind her about the attack." He unconsciously ran a hand over the bump on his head. "I can't say I blame her."

Max nodded in sympathy. "Me neither. Lots of empty bottles in here, too. Can you not recycle these?"

"I'm sure we could, partner," Jamie said. He scooped up a handful of them and dropped them with a resounding *clang* into the dumpster. "It's just a pain in the you-know-what to take them all home and put them in the bin."

What have we here? Max spotted one of the all-too-familiar plastic cases in the mix and opened it up. He glanced at Jamie to see if the man had a reaction to the discovery, but he either didn't care or hadn't noticed what Max held.

Max opened it and saw two small bottles inside. Both contained only a small amount of amber liquid in the bottom. He tossed the container over his head into the trash and scrutinized the bottles. *There are so many bottles I'm becoming suspicious of all of them. It's crazy.*

He stood up to put them in. His foot hit a patch of ice that had been hidden under the powdery snow, and he fell forward. Inexplicably his hand tightened around the bottles, and he landed on the unyielding concrete, smashing them in his hands.

Jamie moved to pull him to his feet and whistled when he saw the bloody mess in the center of Max's palm. "That's nasty, partner. We need to check that out."

"I've got a first aid kit in the gym," Max said. He flicked his hand, flinging blood in tiny strings in the snow. "First my arm, now this. Awesome."

"Doesn't look too bad," Jamie said. "Come on." He led the way to the back door of Tight/Fit and held it open for Max.

Max sent Jamie for the kit in the main workout area, and he went to the bathroom and ran water over his hand. Without the obscuring red mess, the wounds appeared and thankfully didn't look too bad.

"Told you," Jamie said as he set the first aid box on the second sink and opened it up. He pulled on some gloves and lifted Max's hand up to survey it. "This might hurt, partner."

"Just do it," Max said.

Jamie removed a sliver of glass from the center of the palm. "I don't see anymore. That's good. Doesn't look like you need stitches, either." He placed the hand back under the running water. "Dry off, and we'll put some antibiotic and some gauze on it."

"We're all going to be walking around looking like warzone victims before too long," Max said. "I'm surprised one of the news stations hasn't been out here reporting non-stop about all of us crazy people. The walking wounded." He hissed when Jamie rubbed an antiseptic pad over the scratch on his arm. "A little warning would have been nice."

"It's just a little stinging, partner," Jamie chided. "Don't be a pansy." He immediately apologized. "I didn't mean it like that."

Max shook his head. "I know. We're good." He ripped some paper towels from the dispenser and blotted his hand dry.

Jamie caught him when he stumbled sideways a little. "Whoa, it's not that bad. You gonna pass out on me, partner?"

"Just a little dizzy." Max rotated his head in a slow circle and used his undamaged hand to rub his face. "It's probably from lack of sleep, exhaustion, and trying to turn my hand into hamburger. Henny said earlier I looked like I had a tinge of the crud, and she's probably right."

"Maybe. I say when we finish up here, I take you home," Jamie offered. He smeared a dab of ointment on the cuts and began winding sterile gauze around Max's hand.

"Kandy said—Oh, no." He leaned down and threw up in the sink.

"Don't talk. Try not to move. And for God's sake, don't get that on my boots, partner," Jamie said. "Bad enough I have to buy Elaine some new ones. Don't need to throw mine into the mix."

Max nodded and threw up again. He turned on the water and palmed some into his mouth. "I think I'm ready to die now. You finished?"

Jamie tied off his handiwork. "Yup. You gonna make it to the coffee shop, or do I need to get her down here?"

Max took an experimental step with his hand on Jamie's shoulder. "I think I can make it. My stomach is really angry right now, but my head seems to be cooperating. Oh, God!"

He rushed toward the toilet stall and started throwing up before he got there. Jamie held onto him and lowered him to the floor just outside the mess.

"You're hand's on my butt," Max said. He spit into the toilet and started gagging.

"It's nice, but don't flatter yourself too much, partner," Jamie said. "You're not my type."

"Can I convince you to just hold my head under the water until I die?" Max asked.

Jamie laughed. "I doubt it's that bad. You've just got a bug, and need some rest. Seeing all the blood and not having enough sleep are just feeding into it. You'll live."

"I hope not," Max groaned. He spit a few more times. "I think I can make it now."

"Sure? It's easier to clean tile than carpet," Jamie said.

Max pushed himself to his feet, grateful for the assistance. "I'm good. Feeling better already."

"Liar." Jamie steadied him and leaned forward to look at him. "Let me know when you're ready."

"Let's go." Max backed out of the stall, and they made their way to his office. When he finally dropped into his chair, he sighed in relief. "See, I told you."

"You sure did, partner." Jamie held out his hand. "Give me your phone. I'm just going to call Kandy."

Max handed it over and listened in misery to Jamie talking to Kandy. Jamie handed the phone back. "She's on her way. I hope you haven't given me this crap."

"You're all heart," Max said.

Jamie laughed and clapped him on the shoulder. "Elaine thinks so, too.

"William?" Max stared at the man who had almost magically appeared behind Jamie. "What are you doing here?"

"Are you okay?" William moved to Max's side.

Max saw three uniformed policemen standing just outside the door. "What's going on?"

Harris looked at him before turning to Jamie. "Mr. Robertson, I'm afraid you're under arrest for murder and attempted murder."

Chapter Thirty-One

It feels good to be back in business, Max thought. The line at the doors had been longer than he had ever seen for a Monday, especially the Monday before Christmas. *I can't believe it's only two days away.*

Following a couple days of recovering from whatever bug he'd had had been better with Harris at his side. The detective had taken off work to nurse Max back to health, and neither one of them had complained about it.

Max had never been so sick. Thankfully the vomiting had passed quickly, but the nausea and stomach pain had lasted a while. The first morning after getting sick, Harris had had to feed him because he felt too weak to do anything. The detective had even played nurse for changing the bandage on Max's hand.

"Why did you arrest Jamie," Max had asked. He expected Harris wouldn't answer, but was grateful when he did.

"We got an anonymous tip that said he may have been involved in ransacking your gym and stabbing Corey," Harris had said. "We did a search of his business, apparently while he was helping you, and found some things that we felt were enough evidence to implicate him."

"I see. So, does this mean that Bobby is no longer a suspect?" he had asked.

"I'm afraid not." Harris sighed. "There is so much going on in this case. There's nothing clear-cut about it. I can't tell you much because it *is* an on-going investigation. Just please try to be patient. Sometimes these things don't work quickly. Unfortunately."

Unfortunately, Max thought, shaking himself from the remembered conversation.

"Hey, Max, could you take this out to the trash for me?" one of his trainers asked. "I would, but I've got a class starting in like two seconds."

"Sure." He stepped out of the office and took the garbage bag from her.

This time he managed to get out the back door without cutting his arm open. A cold wind slapped him in the face as soon as he stepped outside, and he wished he hadn't left his coat behind.

"You just got over being sick. Are you trying for a repeat?"

He looked to his right, startled by the feminine voice. "Oh, hey, Elaine." Reality quickly set in. "How are you? Have you heard from Jamie?"

She shook her head and hurled her own bag of trash at the stone-grey dumpster. It thudded into the side and fell to the ground. She cursed and moved to pick it up, but Max waved her off and retrieved it instead.

"Thanks," she said. "This is all so crazy. First they think Bobby did it. Now they think Jamie did it. This is tearing the two of us apart, and they don't care." She bit her lip. "I didn't mean Detective Harris, of course."

"It's okay." Max lay his arm across her shoulder and they walked quickly back to the building. "William can't help it that his job doesn't make him many friends. He told me he hated arresting Jamie, especially after he learned what Jamie had done to help me after I got sick. It's just his job."

"I know. Hey, would you come in for a few minutes?" Elaine asked. "I want to give you something."

"Sure." He detoured from the Tight/Fit entrance and followed her into The Vapor Trail. Christmas music played softly overhead, and the smell of pine from a small tree sitting in the middle of the store tickled at his nose.

"I know it's not much, but I thought you might like it," Elaine said. She held out a metallic gold gift bag with glitter-covered white tissue paper poking out the top.

"You didn't have to do this," he said.

"Let's don't do that," she said. "You're going to love it, and Jamie and I want you to have it. Go ahead and open it."

He set the bag on the counter, removed the paper, and pulled out the box sitting in the bottom. "Michael Kors," he said. The fact that his voice was filled with as much awe as someone beholding a masterpiece painting didn't bother him in the slightest.

"It's just cologne, but I knew it would be perfect. Merry Christmas," she said.

"I *do* love it, Elaine. Thank you." He hugged her. "I'll give you your gift tomorrow night at our party. Is that okay?"

"Sure," she said.

He replaced the contents in the bag. "Oh, you decided to give them another try did you?"

She looked down at the boots lying off to the side of the back door and sighed. "Yes. Thankfully they were still in the dumpster. They're nice boots, and I figured I was being silly throwing them away. I got the blood cleaned off, which, I guess, isn't too amazing since I didn't bleed on them that much."

"I'm glad. They look very nice on you." He hugged her again, stepped back out and then into the gym's back entrance.

"Oh, there you are," Barry said as soon as Max came in the door.

"Hi, Barry. How are you and Elizabeth doing?" he asked.

Barry blushed. "We're good. She found a dog she likes, and I think I found someone."

"Good for you. You deserve it. Are you going to be at the party tomorrow night?" Max asked.

"Yes. Is it alright if Elizabeth comes, too?"

"Are you kidding? Absolutely," Max said. "Everyone is really happy for you, and they'll be delighted to see you two together."

"Great," Barry said. His smile was the biggest Max had ever seen. "Oh, before I forget, I found this in the men's room. I'm not sure who dropped it, but I thought you could put it in lost and found."

Max held out his hand, and Barry placed a little black book in it. *I forgot about it!* "Thanks," he said. Whatever Barry's response was, he didn't hear it. *I must have dropped it while I was sick...No, I had it in my back pocket. There's no way it could have fallen out. Jamie! That's why he had his hand on my butt.*

He hurried to his office, put the gift from Elaine on the desk, and flipped quickly through the pages. One had been ripped out, and he realized it was the one with the account number.

What did you not want me to see? What? What? What?

He plopped into his chair and slowly began going down each line of notes and numbers. Page after page, he thumbed through them, seeing scribbled entries about money coming in or going out for various deals. A few lines—marked "Repay costs"—had rather large numbers written beside them.

"Five thousand. Ten thousand," Max said softly. *Skylar was doing some pretty good business. Whoa!* At the top of a page he saw a repayment of $25,000. No dates were in the book anywhere, but Max had a hunch that number coincided with Skylar's meeting Bobby and starting to work at the gym. At the bottom of the same page an entry for "Corey's Pay" was followed by $7000.

"What's this?" Max tilted the book so he could see a line that appeared to be faintly written, but upon closer inspection, he saw that it had actually been erased.

Pulling his phone from his pocket, he activated the flashlight app and shined the light on the page. "Best...night...ever."

Max held the light closer to the page and squinted. "Oh my God!"

Chapter Thirty-Two

"Where do you want this to go?" Max asked. He held up a large platter of finger sandwiches safely shielded by a layer of cling wrap.

"Those go on the long table on the west wall," Kandy said. "Put them there and then come help me get the large coffee carafes down from the top shelf, will you?"

"Sure. How many do you need?" he asked.

"Two, for now," she said. "I've also got eggnog and spiced apple cider for anyone who wants it."

"Eggnog?" He shook his head and made a disgusted face. "Who drinks that crap?"

"Be nice," she chided. "It's Christmas, so let's at least stow the nasty queen attitude and be jolly."

He stuck his tongue out at her. "Well, at least I have my gay apparel on."

"Ha. Ha. You're not funny." She rolled her eyes and disappeared into the back.

"William thought it was funny," he grumbled. He put the tray on the indicated table and followed Kandy to the back. Retrieving the carafes, he filled them and carried them—slowly—to the beverage table.

"Max, would you be a dear and go help John bring the cake over?" Henny asked. "Oh, and while you're there, make sure you grab another fruitcake. I made you an extra one."

"I'm fat enough as it is," he said, kissing her cheek.

She smacked him playfully on the arm. "I'll show you what fat is, you rascal."

He quickly retrieved both items from Crumbles. The cake for the party went on the dessert table, and the fruitcake was tucked safely into the black leather Michael Kors jet-set travel bag Harris had given him as an early Christmas present.

That man spoils me, and I'm okay with that.

"You're thinking about him again, aren't you?" Kandy teased.

Max blushed. "Maybe."

"Don't 'maybe' me." Kandy stopped what she was doing long enough to hip bump him. "I hope you two are happy together. You deserve to be happy."

"Thanks, but we're not officially together. Yet. Speaking of together, did you hear about Barry?" he asked.

"Yes, I can't wait to meet Elizabeth. Contrary to what you've told me, she sounds like a lovely woman," she said.

"It was a Christmas miracle, I'm telling you. I swear I saw her heart grow three sizes that day," Max said.

"You still watch the Grinch?"

"It's a holiday *classic*," he nearly shouted. "It is awesome, and wonderful, and you would enjoy it if you gave it a chance."

"I'm a *Miracle on 34th Street* kind of gal. Sorry."

"You don't look sorry," he said.

"That's because I'm not." Her chuckle became muffled by the wall when she disappeared into the back again.

"Merry Christmas, handsome."

Max turned his smile on Harris. "You, too. Why don't you get something to eat? Everyone else will be here in a few minutes, and then it's going to be like feeding time at the zoo. It's really ugly. You'll enjoy watching it, I promise."

"You're terrible." Harris laughed and made his way to the table to start loading a plate.

The overhead speakers briefly blared the crooning tones of Bing Crosby's *White Christmas* before Kandy got the volume to a level that wouldn't cause permanent damage.

"Sorry," she said to the room at large.

"Merry Christmas, Max." Eden veritably floated across the floor, a brightly wrapped present held out before her. "I know the gift exchange is later, but I really wanted you to have this now."

Max took the small package, weighing it in his hands. "It's pretty heavy." He tore open the paper and pulled the lid off the box inside. "A crystal. Wow, thanks."

"You don't—" Her words were crushed from her by the bear hug he pulled her into. "Well, I'm glad you like it so much." She kissed his cheek and whispered, "It'll help you attune your love energies with those of that delicious detective. Not that I think you need it, but every little bit helps."

He stared, mouth agape, as she fluttered away to the food table. "I *don't* need the help, thanks," he muttered.

One by one, the others all flooded into Mind Your Own Beans, depositing plates or trays of various foods onto the tables. Gifts stacked up under the tree Kandy had put up earlier in the day.

The line for food quickly died away, and everyone had taken their places around the joined tables when the door opened, and a cold wind blew snow inside. A few people shouted. John Gallowylde cursed the mother of the "damned idiot" who had opened the door.

Max looked up and locked eyes with Jamie Robertson. "This is unexpected," he said to Harris before walking to the door. "Jamie, I'm glad you could make it."

Elaine appeared, throwing her arms around her husband and holding him tightly. "How did you get out?"

"Little elves paid my bail," Jamie said. He gently pushed Elaine away. "Go have a seat. I'll be there in a minute." When she was out of hearing, Jamie stepped up close to Max and asked, "What did you tell your boyfriend in order to get me arrested?"

"I didn't say anything," Max said. "It was as much a surprise for me as it was for you."

"I doubt it," Jamie fired back. "I know you want Bobby's name cleared, but I didn't figure on you being low enough to do something like this. I want you to stay away from me, partner. You get me?"

"I didn't do anything," Max said again. "However, while we're at it, why don't you tell me what you did with the page from the black book?"

Jamie didn't bat an eye. "What book?"

"You know which one. The one you pulled out of my pocket while I was puking my guts out."

"It's gone. Don't you worry about it." Jamie clapped him on the back and walked to the table to get his food.

Max sank into his chair and shook his head when Harris gave him a concerned look. "It's okay. He's just mad because he thinks I was the anonymous tipper."

For the most part, the mood was like any other year. Everyone laughed, joked, drank, and ate enough food to make doctors cringe with dread. Max constantly made it a point to avoid looking in Jamie's direction. However, the few times he actually caught the man's eyes, they contained fire slowly building up into a raging storm.

"Everyone, can I have your attention, please." Kandy waited patiently for conversations to die down before she said, "I just want to thank you all for coming tonight. It's been a great year—well, for the most part." She cast a quick glance between Max and Jamie.

Max squirmed in his chair when everyone glanced at him, but Harris's hand on his knee helped center and calm him.

"I hope you've all enjoyed the food, and thank you to everyone who brought things to eat," Kandy continued. "But, we all know that this isn't why we really come here. Let's face it. We're all a bunch of kids and just want some presents. So, let's get to the gift exchange!"

The room filled with shouts, applause, and laughter.

Harris leaned over and whispered in Max's ear. "This should at least put a damper on Jamie's nastiness."

Max looked across out at the obviously angry man and shook his head. "I wouldn't bet your house on that."

Chapter Thirty-Three

Kandy distributed the gifts to everyone. When the last one was received, they took turns each opening one present and thanking the person who had given them the gift. Most were food or nice things that everyone knew the person had wanted. A few were gag gifts that elicited loud, uncontrollable laughter and fire-engine-red embarrassment.

Max watched Jamie sorting through the pile of gifts in front of him, opening one after another—except the one from Max. Finally, he had no choice. He picked up the package, shook it slightly, and stared at Max.

Max said nothing. He just watched—and waited.

Finally, after enough people had goaded him into unwrapping it, Jamie did. The lid to the small white box inside slipped from his fingers and fell to the floor. The screech of his chair on the stone floor matched his indignant shout when he demanded, "What the hell do you mean by this?"

Harris attempted to stand up, but Max said, "No," and the detective sat back down. "So, you do recognize it?" Max asked.

"Of course I—" He stopped, looking briefly at Harris, and shook his head. "I have no idea what you mean. This is just crap—more of your little games to try to pin something on me that I didn't do."

"What do you mean? What does he mean?" Elaine asked Max. "Let me see it."

Jamie snatched the box away. "Leave it, woman. It ain't for you."

She hid her hands in her lap and looked down at them.

Max resisted the urge to stand up. "You didn't get that piece when you removed the other one from the book. Did you see the entry at the bottom?"

Jamie refused to budge. He looked all around the table, and Max couldn't help feeling sorry for the man. *This has to be done,* he thought.

Jamie snatched the paper from the box and scrutinized it. Max could pinpoint the exact second the man's eyes skimmed over the words rewritten in black ink because all color drained from his face. He fell into his chair, shaking off Elaine's attempts to console him.

"I didn't kill Skylar," Jamie whispered, and then he said it louder. "I didn't kill Skylar. As God is my witness, partner, I didn't kill him."

Max stood up, and he felt all eyes in the room instantly on him. He cleared his throat, suddenly nervous, and took a deep breath. "Pretty much everything I'm about to say, I can't really prove," he said. "I probably shouldn't be telling you that, but I have a feeling that's going to be beside the point.

"When I got back from Barbados, I found out a lot of things that had either happened while I was gone, or that I had been too blind to see before I left." He placed his hand on Harris's shoulder, trying to draw strength from him. "One of the first things I learned was about Skylar and Bobby. They'd been having a relationship since I had left.

"The second thing I found out—other than the fact Skylar was dead—was that Corey had been selling drugs out of the gym, and Skylar had been his partner. However, there was a third person involved, the one putting up all the capital, and I think it was you, Jamie."

Everyone glanced back and forth between the two men, muttering to each other. Elaine sat forward in her chair, staring in shock at her husband.

"Everything was going great for a while, until you started getting a little too greedy," Max said. "Then, you told Skylar you wanted a bigger cut of the pie, and that didn't sit too well with him. My guess is he confronted you about it, and you got as mad as we all know you're capable of getting.

"Here was a little fag getting gutsy enough to stand up to you and tell you that he wasn't going to play along," Max surmised. "I don't know much about Skylar Pratt, but I do know that he doesn't take crap off anyone he thinks isn't respecting him."

"It wasn't much more. I just needed the money to make sure the store stayed afloat for a few months," Jamie said. "I'd taken out a big loan to make the initial payment on the drugs we were selling, and I didn't want my supplier coming after me. Or Elaine." He looked at her, shaking his head sadly. "I couldn't endanger her."

"Skylar confronted you about your request, after he informed Corey what was happening, and things took an unexpected turn, didn't they?" Max asked. "By that point, he had figured something out about you."

Jamie locked eyes with Max. "Don't."

"I'm sorry, Jamie, but this needs to be done and said." Max closed his eyes. "As long as I've known you, you have gone back and forth between being either the biggest jackass in the world, or the most vulnerable person I know. You're so quick to take out your anger and point fingers at others so the spotlight gets off you. That's especially true when it comes to gays."

"What are you getting at?" Elaine demanded.

"Jamie's gay, and Skylar found out," Max said.

"What?" Elaine shouted. She pressed her hand over her mouth, shaking her head violently back and forth. "No. Jamie, no. Tell me it's not true."

Jamie refused to look at her. "I can't tell you that, and I'm so, so sorry."

Elaine screamed and pounded her fists onto Jamie's arm until he grabbed her hands and forced them back into her lap. "Please, stop. I know I deserve it, but please stop."

Jamie stared at her a few minutes before saying, "I'd been having…urges. I've always had them, but I thought I could make them go away if I got married and forced myself to love a woman. They just wouldn't go away, and they kept getting stronger. I finally decided I would go to one of the bars in Oklahoma City and see if I could hook up with someone.

"I knew I was sunk when Skylar walked in and saw me." Jamie took a drink of his coffee. "He told me if I didn't have sex with him, he would out me to Elaine and everyone else. So, I did it, and I hate to say this, but it was the most amazing night I've ever had."

"But then Skylar turned the tables again, didn't he?" Max asked.

Jamie nodded his head. "He told me if I didn't pay him, he would tell Elaine what had happened. It was only five thousand dollars—a drop in the bucket compared to what he was making while dealing—but he said it was to prove that I didn't own him—he owned me. I paid it, to shut him up, and tried to just dismiss it as a miscellaneous expense."

"So, *that's* what that money was for?" Elaine demanded. "*That's* why you wouldn't tell me, because your gay lover was blackmailing you?"

"He wasn't my lover," Jamie protested.

"Splitting hairs doesn't make this any better," Elaine shouted. "You have embarrassed me so much."

Jamie didn't acknowledge her words.

"So, after I questioned you about the five thousand dollars," Max continued, "and then I started searching the gym for drugs, you were afraid I was going to find something else that Skylar left, which would reveal your secret. That's why you were in the gym, and why you attacked me."

Jamie nodded. "I didn't aim to kill you, partner. I just needed to get away unseen. I didn't find anything, though."

"Neither did I," Max confessed. "However, after I confronted Corey about his side business, and he told you that I was mad and on a mission for real, you had him ransack the locker room. But, not before you were sure I knew about your involvement because of Kyle's purchase."

"Wait," Harris said. "He was selling drugs out of The Vapor Trail? We didn't find any."

"Of course not," Max said. "After Kyle's purchase, he dumped everything he had and threw all the bottles away in the dumpster. That's what he was doing the day I got sick, and I unknowingly helped him dispose of all the evidence. When you came in, there wasn't anything to find." Max stopped short. "Especially since I may have removed other evidence."

"What?" Harris said.

"I'm sorry," Max offered. "I didn't mean to. Henny came into the store unexpectedly, and I shoved the items into my pants. I couldn't look at the stuff and put it back before Jamie came."

Harris stared at him, and Max mumbled another apology.

"As true as all of this may be," Jamie said, "I did *not* murder Skylar or try to murder Corey. I may be a drug dealer, but I'm not a murderer."

"I know," Max said.

Jamie stared at him, clearly shocked. "If you believe me, partner, why did you have to drag me and my good name through the mud like this?"

"You started out in the mud, Jamie. I'm simply helping you balance out your accounts payable," Max said. "The truth is, the person who killed Skylar also tried to kill Corey, and almost killed me, too."

Chapter Thirty-Four

Harris glared up at Max. "What do you mean the person almost killed you? Why didn't you tell me about that?"

"Because," Max said, "at the time it happened, I didn't realize what was going on."

"How could you not?" Kandy asked.

"I'm getting there," Max promised. "First, let's go back to Skylar. The killer was nowhere near him whenever he died. The police suspected Bobby because he and Skylar had been alone in the gym that morning, and because of a whole lot of other things that tied them together and just made Bobby look like the most convenient suspect.

"Actually, the murder happened a day or so before. Skylar just didn't drop dead until that morning, and nobody realized anything was wrong until it was too late," Max said.

"How is that possible?" Jamie asked.

"Corey and Skylar had started hooking up by the time Skylar blackmailed you into being with him," Max said. "Before Skylar died, Bobby told me that he had gotten very sick. He was throwing up, having stomach cramps, dizziness, and a whole lot of other unpleasant things that were attributed to him having a virus. Kind of like what you thought was wrong with me.

"However, he was actually being slowly poisoned. At first, it was just a little bit, but then he got a really large dose all at once, and that started him toward his death." Max pulled a bottle of clear liquid out of his pocket. "Do you recognize this?"

"It's the liquid pot we were selling," Jamie said.

"Nope. It's actually insulin, and it belongs to Corey," Max said. "He and Skylar were skimming some of their stock and using Corey's empty bottles to store it in. Then, they were using the vaping device to smoke it, just like your actual customers were doing."

"He died from poisoned pot?" Harris asked.

"Nope again," Max said. "He died from nicotine poisoning." He removed the bottle he had found in the case in Jamie's duffel bag. "My guess is this bottle contains a lethal amount of nicotine. It was given to Skylar, who—believe it or not—actually was trying to quit smoking cigarettes. Two more bottles just like it shattered in my hand and poisoned me, too. There just wasn't enough liquid in them to do much more than make me sick.

"But Skylar? He was inhaling it through his vaping device, and it was going straight to his blood stream," Max said. "Bobby thought he had a virus. The next day when Skylar went to work, he had stopped puking, but the secondary effects were just setting in. His heart most likely gave out on him when he was in the sauna, and that, along with the excessive heat, killed him."

"But Skylar got his liquid from me, and I didn't sell him a bottle with a lethal dose in it," Jamie argued.

"No, you didn't, but Elaine did," Max said.

"*What?* That's crazy," Elaine shouted, rocketing to her feet. "I had no reason to kill him. Max, I can't believe you're doing this. Isn't it bad enough you've already destroyed me and my relationship?"

Max sighed and shook his head sadly. "Elaine, I haven't destroyed anything, and I can't let what you did destroy Bobby."

"You can't prove anything," Elaine shouted. "You said so yourself."

"You're right. I did," Max conceded. "However, as shocked as you've tried to act tonight, you already knew that Jamie had slept with Skylar, didn't you?"

"No," she said.

"Yes, you did," Max insisted. "I've seen the pictures in your office. You haven't been happy in a long time, and neither has

Jamie. But then, not too long ago, he started acting *very* happy, didn't he? You hadn't seen him behaving that way since you two started dating. My guess is that when you found out about the five thousand dollars, you rightly assumed that it was to pay off an affair, but you didn't realize it was with a man.

"Like any suspicious wife, you started hunting, looking for anything you could find to accuse Jamie with," Max said. "When you couldn't find anything concrete, you confronted Jamie anyway. He denied it, but you didn't believe him. And then you started noticing how he, Corey, and Skylar spent a lot of time together, and something clicked into place, didn't it?"

Elaine stared at him without saying a word.

"Did Skylar outright tell you he slept with Jamie, or did you guess?" Max asked.

Elaine buried her face in her hands. "He told me," she said through sobs. She cried for several seconds before the tears stopped without warning. "He took great pleasure in telling me every sordid, horrible detail about what had happened. If I could have at that point, I would have killed him where he stood. He ruined my life. He destroyed everything I had worked my whole life to have, and he just laughed about it like it was something he did every day—which he probably did."

"So, you waited until he came to buy more liquid nicotine for his e-cig, and then you gave him the lethal dose," Max said.

Elaine nodded. "And I would do it again. He got what he deserved. I just didn't realize that Corey had the device until I saw you with it the night you helped us with our books. I took it from you, but Jamie found it. When he dropped it in the store, and you gave it back to me, I got rid of it, but I forgot about the other two bottles of nicotine until after…" She looked at Jamie.

"What? Until after what?" he asked.

"Until I saw you and Corey, in the locker room, your arms wrapped around each other while you kissed him like you've never kissed me," she said. Max shivered from the ice in her words.

"I don't remember," Jamie said. "It happened before the attack—" He stopped talking and stared at her. "It was you. You attacked me? You attacked me!"

Elaine laughed. "Of course it was me! When I came out of the store from getting my purse, and you weren't in the truck, I went looking. The gym door was open, so I went in and that's where I saw you and Corey. I was so angry I stabbed him with the collapsible hunting knife you bought for me.

"You were either so shocked or so embarrassed that you ran away. I stabbed Corey while he was stammering that it wasn't what I thought it was. When I left him to die, I found you huddled beside the dumpster, crying like a little baby."

She sneered at him like he was less than human. "I grabbed something from the dumpster and beat you with it until you were unconscious. To make everything fit the story I was coming up with, I ran around to the front and shattered the window.

"By then I realized I had cut myself on the gym's back door when I ran out, so I hit my head on the dumpster and cut myself in the same spot with the knife."

"And most of the blood on your boots was from Corey, wasn't it?" Max asked.

"Yes. I dribbled as much of mine on them as I could and made a point of saying something about it," she said. "Jamie told me you had seen them when he tried to throw them away, so I dug them back out and cleaned them up."

"You also made the phone call to the police about the evidence in Jamie's bag, didn't you?" Max asked.

"Yes," she said. "I thought with that, Jamie would be charged with the murder, and then I could divorce him while he was in prison and save what little bit of face I had left."

Max fell into his chair and looked at Harris. "There's your confession, in front of lots of witnesses. Like I said, Bobby is innocent."

Everyone around the tables stared at Elaine, and she met their eyes unflinchingly. Harris walked around to her, and she stood up without resistance, allowing him to handcuff her and read her rights.

Before she walked out, she looked down at Jamie, "I don't begrudge you the fact that you're gay. You just shouldn't have lied about it or made a fool out of me." She spit on him and left without further incident.

"Excuse me," Jamie mumbled, and he disappeared into the bathroom.

Overhead, Thurl Ravenscroft sang the theme song to *How the Grinch Stole Christmas*.

Chapter Thirty-Five

"Merry Christmas," Max said as he handed a present to Bobby.

"That was last month," Bobby said. "Besides, you proving that I didn't kill Skylar is the best gift you could have ever given me."

Max smiled and squeezed his former partner's shoulder. "It's the least I could do. I'm just sorry you got your heart broken again so soon after we split up."

Bobby sighed. "About that, listen, I'm—"

"We're moving on. *I'm* moving on," Max said. *Tone it down, gorilla man. Don't beat him to death with your words.* "It's okay. We're good. Honestly."

Max sank back into Harris's strong arms. "All things happen for a reason," he said. "At least, that's what I'm choosing to tell myself."

"Okay," Bobby conceded. He hastily unwrapped the box. "Wow, a tablet. That's really cool. Thank you."

"You're welcome," Max said. "I hope you like it. Now, if you don't mind, William and I are going to go have lunch and then head to the airport."

"Enjoy Barbados," Bobby said.

"It'll be nice to see it sober," Max said, laughing. "Not to mention having a hot hunk by my side, too."

He wrapped his hand in Harris's, and together they walked down the sidewalk. The warm, inviting smells inside Mind Your Own Beans enveloped them, and they quickly found a table.

"Hey, guys," Corey said.

"Hey yourself." Max gently hugged him from behind. "That looks amazing. Is it new?" he asked, indicating a sandwich dripping with cheese. The smell of provolone gently wafted up to him. "I know what I'm having."

"Max. Detective Harris." Jamie walked up to the table and sat down across from Corey. "Do you guys want to join us?"

"No, but thank you," Max said.

"Are you two staying out of trouble?" Harris asked.

"I promise, partner," Jamie said.

"Not if I can help it. Ow!" Corey reached under the table to rub his leg. "Why, yes, *officer*, I am being a model citizen," he said in a robotic monotone.

"Good." Harris leaned down and whispered in his ear, "Because if you aren't, and I find out, getting stabbed in the lung will be a picnic compared to what I make sure happens."

"You're a lovely man, and Max deserves you," Corey said. "Max, honey, run."

Max laughed. "The only running I intend to do is along the beach." He looked at Jamie, who was shifting around uncomfortably in his chair. "How's being gay treating you?"

Jamie went pale and looked nervously around the room. "Dang it, partner, I'm still not used to that. You gotta stop."

"Not going to happen," Max said. "I have *years*' worth of crap to catch you up on."

"Max, honey, you're being a fag," Corey said. "It doesn't look good on you. Now, go eat with your delicious boyfriend, and leave mine alone." He shooed the happy couple away.

Max laughed but stopped when he saw the look on Harris's face. "Well, I do owe him a lot of payback," he mumbled.

"That's all well and good," Harris said, "but you should try to be the bigger man and cut him some slack. He's a gay redneck living in a red state. The universe pretty much kicks him enough already, don't you think?" Harris draped his coat over the back of a chair and sat down.

Max sighed and plopped into his own chair. "Fine, but this means you're paying for lunch."

Harris laughed. "Something tells me where you're concerned I'm going to be paying for a lot of things for a *long* time."

Max leaned across the table and kissed him. "And don't you forget it…Willie."

Acknowledgments

Thank you, dear reader, for buying this book and taking time to read it.

I want to thank members of my critique group, *A Murder of Storytellers*, for input and insight. Thank you to Adrean, Ben, Brent, Brooks, CJ, Jack, Kaz, and Kira.

My early beta readers, Jeanne, Laura, Linda, and Rodney offered a lot of encouragement and feedback. Jeanne and Linda caught a glaring mistake in an early draft. Ladies, thank you so much for helping me to not look like a gumshoe.

I also appreciate my end-stage beta readers, Daidria and Tacie. Thank you for your enthusiasm. Daidria, I'm sorry there wasn't more blood.

While all of these people have been involved in the process, please know that any mistakes and inconsistencies are solely mine.

Cover Design by:

TatteredWolf Studios is the joint venture of husband and wife team Brad and Megan Baker (otherwise known as Loni and Tatiyana Wolf). The goal of TWS is to bring their unique design aesthetic to the world through traditional, digital, and video game art.

They can be found at www.TatteredWolfStudios.com.

Other Works by Shannon [Bozarth] Iwanksi

Novel
Ride the Train
Available in eBook or Print at Amazon.com

Short Stories

Finding Annie
Good Morning, Mr. C.
Monsters
All available in the anthology *Happy Days, Sweetheart*

The Dark
Available in the anthology *Beyond the Nightlight*

Upcoming (2015)

A Letter to Die For
Strip Mall Mysteries, Book Two

Short Stories

Afternoon Tea
Available in the anthology *Faed*

Re
The Interview
Available in the anthology *Broken Worlds*

To learn more about Shannon, visit:

www.shannoniwanski.com

www.facebook.com/rttauthor

www.twitter.com/shannon_iwanski

www.ingramcontent.com/pod-product-compliance
Lightning Source LLC
Chambersburg PA
CBHW071240130626
46556CB00003B/1097